THE PREGNANCY PLOT

BY

PAULA

MILLS &
BOON®

First published in Great Britain 2014
by Mills & Boon, an imprint of Harlequin (UK) Limited,
Eton House, 18-24 Paradise Road, Richmond, Surrey, TW9 1SR

© 2013 Paula Roe

ISBN: 978-0-263-90908-1

Harlequin (UK) Limited's policy is to use papers that are natural,
renewable and recyclable products and made from wood grown in
sustainable forests. The logging and manufacturing processes conform
to the legal environmental regulations of the country of origin.

Printed and bound in Spain
by Blackprint CPI, Barcelona

THE PREGNANCY PLOT

As always, my girls, The Coven, without whom
I'd be a blubbering mess of plot confusion on the
floor. But especially to Shannon for that late-night
brainstorming, Deb for the sane wisdom of finishing
the book, and Margie for her brilliant expertise about
fertility treatment and medical procedures.

And a deep, heartfelt thank-you to the man
who inadvertently saved me from my book slump:
British singer, writer and actor Mat Baynton.
Without the wonderful distraction of your show,
Horrible Histories, and the beautiful, inspirational
music that is Dog Ears, this book would have turned
out most different and definitely lacking. You're a
lovely obsession. Thank you more than you'll know.

One

"That bridesmaid keeps checking you out. Do you know her?"

"Who?" Matthew Cooper turned from the huge skyline window, transferring his attention from the stunning seventy-eighth-floor view of Queensland's Surfers Paradise to his sister, Paige. Her familiar teasing grin remained firmly in place as he gave a cursory glance at the impressively decked-out bridal party. The group of six was slowly making the rounds as a glorious sunset illuminated the aptly named Sunlight Room, Q-Deck's premier reception area.

"The redhead," Paige answered.

He shrugged, snagged a glass of champagne from the passing waiter's tray, then went back to the commanding view. "I don't know anyone here. The happy couple are your clients."

Paige frowned. "And you're depressing me. It's a wedding, Matt. A celebration of love. Loosen up a little. Have a bit of fun." She scanned the crowd again. "Go and chat up a bridesmaid."

He raised one eyebrow, jammed a hand into his pants pocket and took a slow sip from his glass. "The redhead?"

"She is *definitely* interested."

Matt murmured something noncommittal.

Paige sighed. "You are one sad guy. Here you are, thirty-six, prime of your life, attractive, single, excruciatingly rich—"

"Responsible. Successful—"

"And still work-obsessed," she concluded as she watched

him check his phone for the third time in half an hour. "I thought you left Saint Cat's to get away from that."

He frowned. "Running GEM is totally different."

"Hmm…" Paige's brown eyes blinked as she popped an appetizer in her mouth, then held up her palms, indicating scales. "On the one hand, heart surgery. On the other, running an international global rescue company." She tipped one hand down, the other up. "Saving lives for the family business—parents overjoyed. Training emergency medical response teams in developing countries—parents pissed off."

"I'm still saving lives, Paige. And I don't need you on my case, too."

"Seeing nasty, lying ex-wife every few weeks." One of Paige's palms dropped. "Skiving off to exotic locations and even more exotic women." Her other hand shot up as she smiled. "Yet you're still not happy."

"I'm—"

"You're not." She touched his arm. "I may live in London but I still know you."

Before he could answer, the bridal party shifted, a solid mass of movement and noise flowing in a singular wave.

It was Friday night in the middle of an unseasonably warm August, and instead of finalizing project details before he flew out to Perth on Monday, he was in a room full of strangers, celebrating the union of two people so obviously in love it was kind of nauseating.

A vague, irrational anger swept over him. The last wedding he'd attended had been his own—and look how that had turned out.

People parted to reveal the newlyweds, Emily and Zac Prescott, sharing a grinning kiss. As the guests cheered, Matthew's jaw tightened, uncomfortable emotions welling in his throat. Why the hell had he agreed to be Paige's plus-one?

"Your ring looks good," he said to Paige, who'd fallen silent.

"As if you can tell from this distance." Still, she visibly

preened as they both studied the intricate, handmade Paige Cooper diamond band on Emily's ring finger. "Look," she added, sharply elbowing him in the arm. "There's the redhead."

The woman in question was partially hidden by Emily's dress. Her head was turned, body angled away so he could only make out the sweep of neck and bare shoulders, the fiery red hair bundled up in a sleek knot at her nape.

Then she moved and a spear of golden sunlight sharpened her profile.

He gasped as everything went out of focus.

"You know her?" Paige asked sharply.

"No. Excuse me for a moment." Ignoring Paige's frown, he shoved his glass into her hand and moved purposely forward.

She was five feet away, lagging behind the rest of the wedding party and talking to a smooth-looking guy. He paused, head spinning as the past flooded in to seize his senses. Angelina Jayne Reynolds—AJ. *Angel,* he'd whispered in her ear, deep in the throes of passion as she'd writhed beneath him. The nickname suited her. From her pale ethereal skin, long elegant limbs and ice-blue eyes, to the deep auburn shock of hair that tumbled down her back in flaming waves, she was a mixture of heaven and hell all rolled into one. A woman who'd set his blood boiling with her joyous laugh and come-hither grin. A woman who'd driven him crazy for six whole months, burned up his sheets, then walked out of his life without a word. It had taken him close to a year to forget that.

But you didn't really forget, did you?

He knew the moment she sensed him staring. Her back straightened and then her shoulders as she scanned the crowd with a faint frown. His gaze remained fixated on her nape, that spot where her gathered hair revealed vulnerable skin. He remembered kissing that spot, making her first giggle in delight, then sigh in rapturous pleasure....

Finally, she turned and the reality of all those missing years slammed into him, making the air whoosh from his lungs.

AJ had been gorgeous at twenty-three. But now she was…
breathtaking. Life and experience had sharpened her features,
accentuating her jaw and chin. Creamy skin and high cheekbones emphasized those blue cat's eyes, the corners slanting
up in a permanent air of mischief.

Then there was her mouth…a luscious swell of warmth and
seduction painted a glossy shade of magenta that conjured up
all sorts of dirty images.

Finally, her gaze met his. It registered brief feminine appreciation, skipped away then snapped back to him in wide-
eyed shock.

He couldn't help but smile.

Somehow, the distance between them disintegrated and he
was suddenly standing right in front of her.

"AJ Reynolds. You look…" He paused, only half aware of
the noise and movement pulsing around them. "Good."

"Matthew Cooper." Her voice came out rushed, slightly
breathy, stirring something he'd buried long ago. "It's been
a long time."

"Nearly ten years."

"Really?"

"Yes."

She threaded her fingers in front of her, the perfect picture
of demureness. He frowned, his eyes skimming over her elegant ice-blue dress, the small butterfly necklace at her throat,
the tiny diamond stud earrings. Something was off.

"You're not used to seeing me dressed like this."

Visions of tangled sweaty limbs and hot breathless kisses
caused a zing of desire to shoot through him. She must've
sensed it because she quickly added, "I mean…the gown."

With an inward curse, he got himself under control. "It is
kind of…"

"Fancy?"

"Elegant."

Her mouth twisted as she glanced fleetingly across the

room. "I know you don't know my sister. So how do you know Zac?"

The bride was her sister? "Through Paige Cooper."

Her eyes widened. "The ring designer?"

"Yes."

"Your wife is very talented." She smiled politely.

"Sister."

"Ah." She glanced at the bridal party, her expression unreadable. "I didn't know you had a sister."

"There were lots of things we didn't talk about."

She simply nodded and smiled at a passing guest, her fingers still threaded in front of her.

Had she ever been this restrained? He remembered AJ as a colorful, passionate talker, using expression and movement to engage. But now it felt almost painfully polite.

Not surprising, considering how they'd parted.

He shoved his hands deep in his pockets.

"Well…" She shot a glance past his shoulder and when he followed it, he spotted Zac and Emily being seated at the bridal table. Off to the side, Paige was deep in conversation with a blinged-out teenager. "It was nice seeing you, Matthew."

"Wait," he said, curling his fingers around her arm. She stilled, her eyes snapping up to his, and he quickly released her. "Can I buy you a drink?"

She gave a slight laugh. "We have an open bar."

"Later." He held her gaze pointedly.

"No, I don't think so," she said, her smile slowly fading.

"A dance, then."

"Why?"

Her directness startled him for one second before he remembered that it was just one of her many appealing traits. "Because I'd like to."

What the hell was he doing? The rational part of his brain was telling him to just let her go. But the unsatisfied, something's-missing part that had survived his marriage's collapse and last week's agonizing new client contract negotiations egged him on.

AJ wasn't a part of his reality. She was a bright memory from his past—an idealistic, purposeful past full of ambition for the future. She was the beach, short shorts, laughter and sensual lovemaking. His present was vastly different. It was endless meetings and lonely foreign countries, the occasional life-threatening situation, a deceitful ex-wife and nosy parents who just couldn't let the past go. He couldn't let her leave. Not yet.

"A dance," he repeated, fixing her with a firm look.

She studied him in silence. Odd. Wasn't this the woman who gave new meaning to *impulsive?* Yet now she seemed downright cautious.

"Matthew, I'm being as polite as possible, given we're at my sister's wedding. But let me make this clear—I do not want to drink or dance with you. Now if you'll excuse me…"

She smiled, then turned on her heel and headed over to the bridal table, leaving him speechless and frowning in her wake.

He glared at her gently swaying backside and the swish of ice-blue skirts billowing around her ankles.

Huh. Guess she's still pissed off with you, then.

Two

Two long hours crawled by, one hundred and twenty agonizing minutes in which AJ wished more than once she still drank alcohol. A champagne buzz would definitely help get her past this irritating awareness of her ex.

His hair is longer, she reflected as she ate dessert. The shaggy style lent a romantic air to his bold features: the wide Roman nose, the dark eyebrows framing dreamy chocolate-brown eyes, the firm jaw shaded with stubble and the dimpled chin. Oh, he was still lean and angular, with elegant hands and expressive eyes that reminded her of chivalrous knights and romantic poets from days gone by, but in those ten years he'd broadened and matured. It suited him.

Not only was he gorgeous and hyper-smart, he was also a doctor. An actual heart surgeon, for heaven's sake, every girl's McDreamy with a deep, soothing English accent that made her shiver. Yet no TV character could hold a candle to the reality that was Matthew Cooper.

Maybe it was the memory of their mutual past. A past based purely on sex—they hadn't been together long enough to crash and burn under the weight of inevitable relationship complications. Instead, Matthew had brutally cut her off at the knees.

Amazingly, she made it through her toast and then the official bridal party dance without a hitch. Her partner dutifully waltzed her around the dance floor as Zac and her sister glided by, smiling and whispering in that enviously intimate way of all newlyweds.

Eventually the DJ cranked up the music, the lights dimmed and everyone flocked to the dance floor. After refusing to dance with a chisel-jawed blond, she made her way to the bar and ordered a virgin cocktail.

"Having a good time, gorgeous?" The bartender grinned.

"Sure." She smiled halfheartedly.

He placed the drink in front of her, but when she reached for it his hand lingered, his gaze intent. "Hey, what do you say to—"

Suddenly Matthew was there, easing onto the stool next to her, his polite smile aimed directly at the bartender. It was almost funny the way the other man yanked his hand away and quickly asked, "What can I get you, sir?" But when the bartender went to fix a coffee and Matt turned to face her, amusement was the last thing on her mind.

After the year she'd had, she was so not up to facing the man who'd dumped her nearly ten years ago.

AJ stared into her drink, watching the bubbles rise to the surface as she stirred it with the straw. She'd been good enough to have hot holiday sex with but not good enough to introduce to his parents or take out on an official date. To advertise as girlfriend material.

Ah, but it *had* been amazing sex.

The memories made her cheeks flush. With a small sigh she shoved the straw between her lips and took a sip, ignoring his gaze.

The bartender placed the coffee on the bar—espresso, no sugar—and her eyes were drawn to Matt's long fingers curling around the cup. His scrutiny was beginning to unnerve her. Sure, he'd always been intense, examining things from every possible angle. It was part of what made him such a brilliant surgeon. But this…this…singular attention, as if he couldn't quite believe what he was seeing, was something different.

"Stop staring. I haven't changed *that* much," she finally said, irritated.

"You have." He lifted the cup to his lips and took a chug, then carefully replaced the cup on the saucer.

"How?"

One eyebrow went up. "Fishing for compliments, AJ?"

"No."

His expression changed. "Yeah, I remember that about you. You look…" He paused, and an inexplicable rush of anticipation stilled AJ's breath. "Thirty-two suits you," he finally said. "Very much."

Oh. Perversely disappointed, she took another sip of her drink and smiled politely. "Thank you."

"So how've you been?"

If you don't count my surgery, my screaming biological clock and the fertility clinic appointment tomorrow? "Fine." She eased off her chair and smiled once more, only this time it felt as if her face was about to crack. "Well. It was nice seeing you. Again. I—" When he muttered something under his breath, she frowned. "Sorry?"

"I said, crap. What the hell's gotten into you, AJ? It wasn't 'nice' seeing me again and you know it. So stop faking."

AJ took a step back and crossed her arms, trying to rein in her irritation. "You know what? I'm not doing this with you. Not here, not now." And she abruptly turned and stalked off.

Her heels barely made a sound on the stucco dance floor, the thumping music drowning out everything except the anger in her head. She managed to dodge a handful of dancers, then a tipsy guest, before making it through an archway at the far end of the room. With a vicious yank she pulled a door open and stepped inside the luxurious foyer that led to the restrooms.

Pausing at one of the full-length mirrors, she stared at her reflection, then cupped her cheeks, heat flaring beneath her palms.

Matthew Cooper was an arrogant ass. He was a trust-fund kid with upper-crust parents and a British ancestry dating back to the Battle of Hastings. An insanely intelligent silver-

spooner who never knew what it was like to truly struggle…
for a life, for control, for his next meal. He was the most self-
centered, overbearing—

No. This wasn't about him. Her life had been one insane
rollercoaster ride since April: in the space of a week she'd
gone from her normal checkup to being prepped for surgery
to remove ovarian cysts. Determined to keep Emily's happy
prewedding bubble intact, she'd told no one, but her luck had
run out when she'd run into Zac at the hospital, where he'd
been donating some huge sum to the children's ward and she'd
been coming out of post-op. She'd sworn him to secrecy, but
then the rat had insisted on paying for everything, including
a week's recuperation at a private health facility.

*It's highly unlikely you'll be able to bear a child, Miss
Reynolds.*

Oh, her surgeon had his sympathetic bedside manner down
pat, and a few years ago she would've brushed off his concern
with barely a backward thought. The mere idea of *her*—Miss
Single Girl, Life of the Party—having kids was laughable,
right? Her fractured childhood notwithstanding, she loved the
fact she could pick up stumps and move across the state on a
whim, answering to no one, depending on no one and needing no one. Sure, there were those weird little pangs when
she saw Emily and Zac together and she briefly yearned for
something more. And it seemed like all her friends were dropping off her radar one by one, suddenly engrossed in getting
married, falling in love or having babies.

Not AJ Reynolds. She didn't need anyone.

Except now, the most basic choice of womanhood had been
ripped from her and the sudden, inexplicable loss gaped like
a jagged wound.

She'd started to question all the turns she'd taken to get to
this point, every minute choice she'd made. That unfamiliar
self-scrutiny had freaked her out, but finally, after a week of
agonizing, she'd woken up one morning and known exactly
what she wanted.

The heavy sucking sound of the door opening, followed by a sudden brief burst of music and laughter, broke through her thoughts. She narrowed her eyes at Matthew's reflection in the mirror, refusing to turn around even when the silence lengthened and her skin itched with expectation.

"The men's room is next door," she said helpfully.

He ignored her comment. "You're still angry with me."

She whirled, ready to do battle, but took a calming breath at the last moment.

"Being angry means I still care." She tipped her chin up, giving him her best down-the-nose glare, even though he was a good six inches taller. "And I don't."

"Right."

His superiority grated. "Oh, get over yourself, Matt! It's been ten years. I've moved on. Grown up. I'm living my life. You…" She waved a hand, taking in his perfectly suited frame. "You're probably married to some socialite, chief of something by now and pleasing the pants off your parents—"

"Actually, I'm divorced and run an international medical response team."

"—and honestly, I don't think—" AJ paused then blinked. "What?"

"I run GEM. It's a global emergency medical—"

"Wait, wait, wait. You *quit* Saint Catherine's?"

He nodded. "Just over four years ago."

AJ was stunned. "Holy crap. But you lived and breathed that place. It was your entire existence and you… Wow. What did your parents say?"

"Considerably more than 'wow.'" The cloud in those hooded velvet eyes spoke volumes, belying the casual quirk of his lips.

"Wow," she said again. He remained silent as she stared at him.

He'd been married. It was old news, but her heart still smarted. He'd loved someone enough to propose. He'd taken someone else to bed and been loved in return.

Was it wrong to hate someone she didn't know?

AJ focused on his beautiful mouth. She knew the second his thoughts solidified: his brown eyes darkened, nostrils flaring as he slowly dragged in a breath. "Angel…"

She swallowed. "Don't call me that."

She heard a loud click and jumped as the room was suddenly plunged into pitch darkness.

The light timer had run its course. With a soft curse, AJ stuck out her hands and took a step forward.

"AJ?"

"I'm walking to the wall." She took another step, then another…until she found something solid. And warm. Definitely *not* the wall.

She sprung back with a dismayed groan and would've lost her footing if not for Matt's quick response. He grabbed her arms, steadying her. "I've got you."

"I'm fine."

"Yes, you are." The blackness was absolute but she could still hear the smile in his voice.

Her breath hitched as his hands seared her skin. "You can let go now."

"Okay."

But he didn't. Instead, he cupped her elbows and suddenly every one of her senses went on high alert.

His long sensual fingers were warm on her skin and his subtle scent beckoned. When she felt him shift, a wave of body heat swathed her, drawing her into a seductive web.

Damn it. Her heart pounded in familiar anticipation. She heard him draw in a breath, then slowly exhale. That gentle puff of air was way too close to her cheek.

"Matthew. Turn the light on."

"I will."

"Now."

"You *are* still angry."

"That doesn't concern you." She struggled in his grasp so that when he released her, she crashed into his chest and her lips collided with his.

She gasped and pulled back, a second too late. That fleeting moment of delight had done its job.

The door suddenly swung open, and the light automatically switched back on. They both blinked and turned to see Paige standing in the doorway.

Everyone froze in a strange tableau of embarrassment, followed by an immediate gathering of dignity as AJ and Matt both sprang apart.

"Oh, hey," Paige said, way too casually. "I've been looking for you everywhere, Matt. The newlyweds are leaving. You want to go?"

"In a minute." But he stayed where he was, studying AJ so thoroughly that she ended up smoothing down her perfectly straight skirts with nervous fingers.

AJ didn't miss the way Paige's speculative gaze swept over them or the small grin on her lips. *Oh, great.* "I should be going, too."

"We could share a cab if you want," Paige said.

"Oh, I still have the bridal car…."

"Really?" As Paige's face lit up, AJ groaned inwardly. *Damn.*

"You could share with me, if you like," she said reluctantly. *Say no, say no, say no.*

"That'd be great! Wouldn't that be great, Matt?"

His gaze darted from AJ to his sister, and a small frown suddenly furrowed his brow. Then he stuck his hands in his pockets and shrugged. "Wonderful."

At the last minute, Paige conveniently realized she'd forgotten her purse. With an "I'll just grab a cab—don't worry!" she slammed the door on their surprised expressions and the Bentley pulled away from the curb.

The silent drive was awkward. AJ kept her legs crossed, her body angled toward the door, her gaze firmly out the window, but it still didn't stop her from casting furtive glances at Matt's reflection in the glass.

There was something about *this* man, this one particular person with whom she'd shared her body so freely and willingly. Out of all the other guys, she'd actually liked this one. He had ample cause to be a complete jerk—money, breeding, genius-level IQ, brilliant career, lush looks. But he wasn't.

At least, not until *that* night. And to be fair, she'd read far more into their fling than she should've. A mistake she'd avoided making for years afterward. Until Jesse.

She shook her head, refusing to think about her last stupid mistake. Instead, her thoughts wandered back to Matt. Who knew what had shaped him in those ten years? Something obviously huge, considering he'd thrown away a career he'd sacrificed everything for since high school.

Matthew finally broke the silence. "So what are you doing now?"

Crashing and burning. Feeling way too attracted to you. Wanting to touch— "Going to my hotel."

"I meant for work," he replied patiently.

She sighed and slowly turned to him. This was her punishment for bad judgment—death by small talk. "I have a stall at the Gold Coast markets."

"Selling what?"

"Drawings."

"You draw?"

"And paint. I even do a pretty good caricature, which is my best seller."

"I didn't know you were an artist. I mean," he amended, "I saw you sketching once, but…"

"We just shared a bed, Matt, not our deepest thoughts about life and love." She shrugged. "We had fun for a few months."

She remained surprisingly calm under his scrutiny, even though her insides jumped as his fingers softly drummed on the door.

You're not twenty-three anymore. You can hold a man's gaze without backing down like a blushing virgin.

"We had fun," he repeated slowly.

The heat of irritation crept up her neck. "Well, *I* did."

His eyes darkened, mouth tilting into a knowing grin. "I know. I was there, remember?"

Unfortunately she'd been doing nothing but remembering ever since she'd clapped eyes on him. And if she were the old AJ, the one who'd lived and loved with careless abandon, she wouldn't hesitate to follow through. Judging by the sensuous curl of his mouth and the way his gaze devoured her, he was thinking the same thing.

She took in his lopsided smile and the tiny dimple it made, the way his eyes roamed leisurely over her face and hair before coming to rest on her mouth. The way those eyes then darkened with a predatory gleam.

Growing up, she'd quickly learned how to read peoples' expressions, predict a mood then act accordingly. This skill had been a good foil for her smart mouth, which had provoked the bulk of her mother's slaps. That little girl desperate for a mother's love was long, long gone.

The message she saw in Matt's eyes was plain as day. He wanted her. And judging by that smile, he was reading her need as easily as the Sunday sports section.

It seemed he was about to say something more but instead glanced out the window. AJ followed his gaze, to the blazing lights of the Phoenician. Her time was up.

"This is my stop," she said unnecessarily, her smile tight. "Well, goodbye. Have a safe trip back to Sydney."

"Thanks."

She eased from the car and, to her surprise, he followed.

"I'm perfectly capable of seeing myself to my room," she said tartly.

He lifted his hand, her thin handbag strap dangling from one finger. "You know, that hairstyle really doesn't suit you."

She grasped her bag strap. "I'm supposed to be a demure bridesmaid."

He refused to relinquish the bag. "Demure?"

She watched his gaze go past her shoulder to the people coming and going from the hotel. "Give me my bag."

With a small tug, he drew her closer. "I'm staying at the Palazzo Versace. Have lunch with me tomorrow."

Her heart leaped for one second before she ruthlessly shot down that eager spark. "No."

"You have something else planned?"

"Yes."

"You can tell me more about your paintings."

Oh, you are smooth, Matthew Cooper. From his languid, willpower-melting smile to the way his head tilted, she knew *he knew* she was attracted. She'd made some colossal mistakes in her past, but denying her body's desires was not one of them.

How long had it been?

Too long. A familiar sliver of excitement prickled just before she sighed and tugged at her bag again. In response, he tightened his grip and tugged back.

"Damn it, Matt, give me my—"

He took her hand and threaded his fingers through hers. The gentle slide of warm flesh, the firm conviction as he curled his hand around hers had her blood leaping to life.

Matthew had beautiful hands, with smooth sun-darkened skin and lean fingers. Perfect surgeon's hands, miracle instruments of power and talent, whether he was performing intricate lifesaving surgery or bringing her to a panting climax.

Her breath gurgled in her throat.

He began to stroke her knuckles with his thumb. That shockingly personal intimacy did her in, scattering all rational thought.

Then he firmly drew her forward and, in the middle of the hotel entrance in front of a dozen milling guests, placed a kiss square on her mouth.

Alarm made her pulse skyrocket, yet familiar desire dissolved any objections. His mouth was as warm and skillful as she remembered. Her whole body took barely a second to recover, to remember, then it was off and running, eager for more as her eyes fluttered closed and she kissed him back.

She didn't care that his lips curved into a knowing, way-too-confident smile beneath hers. All she could think of was that mouth, tasting of coffee and something forbidden, urging hers wider, devouring her; then his tongue as he gently eased her open and dove inside.

Damn him. He knew how to turn a woman on.

A group of hotel guests abruptly surrounded them, cheering and whistling, edging past with alcohol-infused enthusiasm and bringing with them movement and noise and sudden clarity.

She pulled back and Matthew reached out to steady her, his breath warm across her cheek. When their hips bumped, then their shoulders, a frisson of delight shivered up her spine.

AJ barely noticed the brief, cheerful apologies as the crowd moved on. All she noticed were Matthew's warm palms cupping her elbows, his soapy-fresh scent and his breath as it feathered across her bare shoulder.

"Want to change your mind about me seeing you to your room?" he murmured in her ear, his deep accented baritone making her nerves dance.

"No."

He grinned. "So lunch tomorrow?"

"Contrary to popular belief, the world doesn't revolve around you, Matthew Cooper." She dug in her bag for her phone and checked the time. "I have things to do tomorrow."

"Dinner, then."

She sighed. Sharing food with him, making small talk, was the last thing on her wish list, especially after her appointment tomorrow.

He reached out and took her phone. She scowled. "What are you—?"

He flicked it on and dialed. "Here's my number." He paused and his phone trilled from somewhere inside his jacket. Then he returned hers. "Lunch tomorrow."

With a confident grin, he turned and strode back to the car. She glared at his broad back. *Of all the arrogant…*

The Bentley finally drove off. With a sigh, she turned on her heel and walked into the hotel foyer. This wasn't a problem. She'd just call tomorrow and cancel. There'd be nothing he could do about it, after all.

Yet it didn't stop the niggling feeling that she was throwing away the chance to have Matthew back in her bed again.

Irritated, she punched the elevator button. Sure, she'd lusted. She'd wanted. She'd desired. But she'd never completely offered him her heart and he'd never demanded it. She'd been young and reckless, reveling in life, and he'd been the perfect fling. Yet despite her oh-so-mature outlook on the whole affair, he'd still managed to bruise her.

Matthew Cooper was part of her past, not her future. If she was an expert at anything, it was moving on and letting the past stay buried.

Three

AJ perched on the edge of her chair in the discreet Brisbane fertility clinic, hands clasped firmly in her lap.

She'd managed to get a grasp on her emotions, wrapping them with prudent caution. Yet she couldn't stop the edginess that rose up, catching her breath and making her heart kick.

Forget about Matthew Cooper and just get on with your original plan.

Dr. Sanjay flicked open the file on his desk. "How are you today, Miss Reynolds?"

"Fine. Nervous."

He looked up from the file and peered over his glasses with a smile. "So, this is your second consult. Dr. McGregor did your full checkup and discussed the realities of getting pregnant with you?"

"Yes."

He kept reading. "It says here you had surgery three months ago for ovarian cysts."

"Yes, my surgeon did say my chances of conception were low. Thirty percent."

"You have quite a bit of scarring—"

"But thirty percent is better than nothing, right?"

He sighed, then gave a reluctant nod. "It doesn't mean it's impossible—just difficult. But it will be time consuming, and fertilization may not happen the first, second or even the fifth time. And it can be draining, physically, mentally and

financially." He glanced back down at the file. "You've already chosen a donor from our files, I see."

She nodded.

"Okay." Sanjay flipped open the file, then frowned. "One
moment." He reached for the phone and made a call. When
he hung up, he slowly removed his glasses, closed the folder
and fixed her with a silent, considering gaze.

Uh-oh. She nervously twisted the handles of her handbag.
"What's wrong?"

"Miss Reynolds, I'm sorry but we cannot proceed at this
time."

Her mouth gaped. "Why not?"

"I've been advised your donor is no longer available." He
gave her a sympathetic smile.

"What?"

"Your donor cancelled his appointment," Sanjay said
calmly. "This means—"

AJ stared blankly at the manila folder as the doctor's explanation faded into the background. No. *No!* This could *not*
be happening.

"Miss Reynolds?" the doctor repeated gently. "Did you
hear me? How do you want to proceed?"

"What do you mean?"

He paused, silently studying her as if trying to assess her
mental state. "You'll need to make another donor choice and
then we can go from there. You'll need to make another appointment with reception."

He slid a business card across his desk, almost as if he'd
been waiting for the cue, but all she could do was stare at him.
"But…but…I don't… It took me three months to get this one!
Can't I just—"

"I am sorry about the long wait time but we are fully
booked. And I am legally bound to follow procedure." He
straightened the files on his desk, then fixed her with a polite
smile. "You need time to make a decision and once you have,

we can discuss everything at our next appointment. Now, can I help you with anything else?"

AJ shook her head and took the card, her fingers surprisingly steady.

When she finally strode outside, the bright morning sun seared away the vague clinical aroma and the doctor's sympathetic but hands-tied expression. Slipping on her sunglasses, she crossed the road to the parking lot and dug out her phone.

She found her car—a third-hand, beat-up red Hyundai Getz—and slipped into the driver's seat.

Just what was she going to do now?

She stared at the cracked steering wheel, her mind a total blank. Another three months. Could she wait that long? She'd done her research—she knew anxiety and worry played a huge factor in getting pregnant. And there was no guarantee the first time would work anyway. She'd been on a dozen different blogs and forums where women openly shared their stories—the injections, the schedules, prime ovulation times, family pressure, aching optimism and the deep, dark lows of constant negative tests. She'd read about women making the agonizing choice of stopping fertility treatments after years of stress, only to fall pregnant months later when the pressure was off. Her head had spun with overload.

She could spend years chasing this dream. And where would she get the money? She'd never had a loan in her life and there was no way she'd stoop to sponging off Emily. Big sisters looked out for the little ones; they didn't demand handouts.

Her mind was a whirling mass of chaos, thoughts flying everywhere, so it took a few seconds to realize her phone was ringing. Confused, she finally grabbed it and stared at the screen.

Her sharp laugh shattered the still air. It was Matthew. Great.

"Yes?"

"Just checking you'll be here for lunch."

His deep voice, combined with that polished accent, sent her thoughts into further turmoil. She glanced at her watch. Ten o'clock. It felt like she'd been in there for hours. "Probably not. I'm in Brisbane."

There was a pause. "Later, then. The Versace does an exceptional high tea."

She opened her mouth to refuse, but a sudden insidious thought struck her speechless.

Oh. My. God.

She shook her head. *No.*

But wait! What if...? No, you can't.

Sure, you can.

She took a deep breath, then another.

"AJ?"

"I'm thinking," she replied, dragging a hand through her hair.

"Don't take too long," he murmured. "Time's ticking away."

Never a truer word was spoken. Her forbidden idea slowly took shape. Matthew Cooper had the power to grant her most desperate wish. He was the perfect male specimen. The perfect candidate. The key to her plan.

Matt could give me a baby.

Yes! No! Indecision warred inside before she finally overrode her doubts and chose a side.

"I'll be there at one," she said and turned the key in the ignition.

Matt hadn't actually expected her to say yes. Now, as he waited in the Palazzo Versace's opulent coffee lounge, he wondered if this was such a good idea.

His entire life was a study in cool-headed decision-making. He made plans, logical moves, well-informed choices. Choices that had furthered his career, challenged his intellect and increased his standing in the medical community. And when he'd reached his personal crisis point, that cool head had led him to a new calling.

Yet he'd impulsively asked AJ out. In the space of an evening, she'd managed to rub off on him.

Hell, he never could control himself around her.

He shook his head and glanced over at the reception area for the fifth time in as many minutes. Circular couches with plump sun-yellow cushions were scattered throughout the foyer and the sleek, intricately tiled marble entrance bore the familiar Versace logo. Some said this five-star Gold Coast hotel blurred the line between lavish and garish, but he loved it. It was private, the staff was discreet and service was top-notch. He never stayed anywhere else when he was in Surfers.

He glanced up again, and when he spotted a familiar figure walking through the huge glass doors, her low strappy heels clicking sharply on the tiled floor, his thoughts fled like pre-dawn shadows at sunrise.

He'd recognize that distinctive red hair anywhere, even if it was tied back in a controlled ponytail. He also noticed how her brow was furrowed in concentration.

AJ had a habit of frowning when she didn't agree with what was being said, those tiny disapproving lines momentarily creasing her forehead before she opened her mouth and began challenging, questioning.

She may look like a Renaissance painting, but her brain was firmly twenty-first century.

He ran his eyes over her, taking in the beacon of hair, the soft lemon cardigan over a modestly cut cream sundress, the silver sandals on her feet. She looked…demure. Again. A word he'd never consider for a woman who'd worn screaming-orange and electric-blue with impunity, who'd rocked short denim shirts and sexy off-the-shoulder tops, who laughed and loved equally with impulsive, joyous abandon.

Burning curiosity sparked in him as he strode across the foyer.

When she finally noticed his approach, a smile replaced her frown. It was all-encompassing, defining those high cheekbones and creasing her clear blue eyes. It felt as if he was the only guy in the world and she was smiling just for him. And yeah, it also jammed the words in his throat as if he were a boy with his first crush.

Irritating and arousing—that was AJ to a T.

So he did the only thing he could—smiled in return, took her arm and placed a kiss on her cheek. She stilled in surprise, and he immediately pulled back, decorum warring with craving.

"How…?" She swallowed then went on breathily, "How are you?"

Suddenly needing to do more than kiss your cheek.

"Hungry. Are you?" he asked thickly.

"Not particularly."

As soon as the words were out of her mouth, AJ sensed the danger. It was like fire crackling to life, flaring up to bathe her in delicious heat. His eyes were dark, full of forbidden promise, and suddenly AJ recalled another time, another place, where they'd forgone food and instead feasted on each other until dawn crept into the sky.

She dropped her gaze.

His palm cupped her elbow in a soft caress. "I've arranged for us to eat outside. Come."

She let him lead her past the huge windows with a view of a massive, Greco-Roman-style pool and fountains sparkling in the afternoon sun, then out the doors. A bead of sweat formed in the small of her back, and she slipped her sunglasses on. The water looked so inviting.

"Have you been here before?" he asked, his hand a warm brand on her as they wove their way through the pristine cabanas ringing the pool.

"Once, for dinner." Zac and Emily had treated her, and she'd spent the whole time stroking the chair and lusting after the dinner plates.

They stopped in front of a cabana, where a female server greeted them. "Good afternoon, Dr. Cooper. Your afternoon tea is ready. Would you like me to serve you now?"

"No, that's fine. Thank you." When he smiled, AJ swore she saw a blush rise in the girl's cheeks before she nodded and left them.

Their private air-conditioned cabana looked like a sheikh's tent. She glanced around, noting the cotton-draped walls and roof and the table on the far side that held coffee and tea jugs warming on heating plates. A love seat against another wall was scattered with a dozen cushions displaying the distinctive Versace pattern. Two recliners flanked a low table that held an elegant three-tiered display of sweet and savory treats that made AJ's mouth water.

Matt nodded to the chairs. "Take a seat."

She hesitated, then toed off her shoes before settling into the lounge with a sigh. After her crazy morning this was a welcome respite, despite Matt's surreal presence amid the luxurious five-star hotel aura.

He took a seat across from her at the low table. She focused on the spread before them.

"Is that smoked salmon? And cream cheese?"

"Your favorite, right?"

She sighed. "You always knew how to make me smile, Matthew Cooper."

His mouth grazed her bottom lip before he reached for her coffee cup and began to fill it. "I'm planning on doing much more than that."

Oh, wow. She didn't care that her answering grin was full of girlish giddiness, nor that anticipation made her hand tremble as she took her cup.

"Really." She took a sip, eyeing him over the rim.

"You told me you hated playing games, remember?" He met her firm look with one of his own. "I'm just being honest."

Yes, he was. She looked away, unable to hold his gaze any longer. *Here's your chance. Ask him now.* She replaced her cup and reached for a tiny smoked salmon sandwich. "So how long were you married?"

He paused, a sliver of bread roll halfway to his mouth. "Does it matter? It's over."

"It doesn't." She shrugged. "I'm just curious."

"Her name was Katrina," he finally said, then popped the food into his mouth and slowly chewed. "We were married for three years. You?"

"Oh, no. Not me." A memory flashed by, but she swallowed the bitter ashes with a neutral expression as she selected another morsel from the platter. "And you left Saint Cat's." She nibbled on the finger sandwich. Chicken and pesto—delicious.

"To start my own company."

But why? The question hovered on her tongue but she swallowed it back. Did she really need to know?

She took a sip of coffee, studiously avoiding his gaze as she finished the chicken and pesto, then picked a mini chocolate croissant. She bit into it and gave a small murmur as the buttery pastry crumbled in her mouth.

"Good?"

"Oh, yeah."

"I thought you'd like it."

"Oh, you did?" She licked her bottom lip, picking up a stray crumb. And just as she expected, Matt's gaze honed right on in, watching her as she slowly licked one finger, then her thumb.

Her breath staggered on the intake. There was nothing to stop her from leaning over the table and suggesting she was hungry for something more than food. Hell, this cabana was just as good as a private room—they could get naked right here, right now, and no one would suspect a thing.

Yet something made her hesitate. This was Matt. The guy she'd shared a bed with for six whole months. The guy she'd been prepared to let down all her defensive walls for, only to be dumped that same night. The guy who'd been her benchmark, who'd made her vow never to be that vulnerable again.

"Matt…" she began, then paused when he abruptly stood. He was staring down at her with such intensity that the rest of her words gurgled in her throat. She knew that look. It still made her legs weak even after all these years.

"Come with me."

When he rounded the table and held out his hand, she was lost.

His fingers wrapped firmly around hers, slowly drawing her to her feet, to him. Her heart hammered as she stared into those dark eyes, that crazy feeling of anticipation simultaneously scaring and exciting her.

Kiss me.

As if she'd spoken aloud his eyes dipped, then his head, and everything fell out of focus. She felt her eyes close, the familiar arousal bubbling up in her belly. Yet when he was barely a breath away, when her senses were full of his delicious scent, her breath ragged and her belly tight, he stopped.

She'd been leaning in, practically begging for him to kiss her. With a small sound of frustration, she opened her eyes and saw him grinning.

Then he turned and pulled her with him.

They left the cabana in silence, her shoes forgotten as they moved swiftly past the pool. AJ barely had time to register the scorching hot tiles beneath her feet before they were inside the cool foyer, Matt leading her to the long bank of elevators. He pressed the button and then looped his arm around her waist, pressing his warm body into her back.

His solid heat made her mind reel. It had been too long since she'd been this intimate with a man. She'd missed having a pair of strong arms hold her, a hot hard body intimately pressed against hers.

When the elevator pinged open, they rushed inside. He swiped his card, then turned to face her when the doors slid smoothly shut.

And she was staring right back at him.

He was tall, well over six feet, and although she was hardly short, her shoulder barely reached his bicep. She caught a glimpse of her reflection in the elevator mirrors—

conservative hairstyle, demure dress. Hardly the outfit for a seductress, yet he'd—

He swooped in and kissed her.

It was a hot, determined kiss designed to awaken and arouse, a kiss she recalled stirring her from sleep and into full-blown desire in seconds flat. It was just as good—no, even better than—last night. Her fingers curled around his biceps and the tension in those muscles matched the scorching pressure of his mouth. He took fierce control, forcing her mouth open, and with a squeak of surprise she let him in. Everything throbbed—her skin, her pulse, her groin. His arousal pressed between them, a hard reality against the thin barrier of their clothes.

"Angel," he breathed. AJ groaned as memories engulfed her. It was the one word he'd always whispered when he brought her to climax again and again.

She barely registered the elevator had come to a stop. Matt suddenly pulled back, spinning her to face the front with a wicked gleam just before the doors slid open.

An elderly woman got on and AJ murmured a polite greeting, her face warm and her blood pounding. Matt was standing behind her, his hands stuck casually in his pant pockets, studying the glowing numbers as they continued their ascent. Yet his thigh nestled firmly against her bottom, heat searing through her thin dress.

She stared at the slowly changing floor numbers until her nerves felt so tight they began to scream.

What on earth do you think you're doing?

She never dwelled on the past or rehashed it. Moving on was what she did, what she'd always done. She'd come to terms with it all, had matured, grown.

So why was she still thinking about it?

She'd been twenty-three. They'd both gone into their affair with a mutual understanding it was only temporary. Of course his career had come first. Saint Catherine's up-and-coming neurosurgeon didn't belong with an addict's daughter and runaway thief.

When their fellow passenger got off on the tenth floor, AJ took an unsteady breath. *I am me. AJ Reynolds. I am not the broken product of those awful people. I have a sister who loves me. I have friends. I am smart. I love animals. I don't cheat or lie. I'm a good person.*

So would a good person manipulate and seduce to get what she wanted?

Matt gently urged her forward, breaking into her thoughts. She glanced up to see they'd reached the top floor just before the doors quietly opened onto the long plush hallway.

Sweat popped out in the small of her back. She could feel the tickle as it slowly slid down, down, until her dress eventually absorbed it.

"AJ?"

She squeezed her eyes shut as his hand cupped her hip, the familiar firmness creating alternate bursts of doubt and desire in her belly.

You can do this.

The corridor was way too long, its walls adorned with exclusive hand-drawn Versace designs in gilt frames. Then finally they were at his door, a huge, dark wooden thing emblazoned with a fresco of classic Greek gods and a gold number three. He opened it with his card and she caught her first glimpse of the amazing decor inside the cavernous penthouse suite along with a sliver of blue sky from the huge patio windows. As she hesitated at the threshold, he gently pulled her against him. Her bottom connected with his groin and his lips went to her nape.

She gasped. With one hand braced on the door frame, he looped the other low across her belly.

"I want you in my bed, Angel," he murmured in her ear, his hot breath and rough stubble sending tiny waves of longing over her skin. "I want to have you beneath me, above me, around me."

He shifted, the truth of his arousal solid against her butt.

Sinful memories flooded in to hijack her senses. In his pool, slick and hot in the moonlight. On the beach at sunrise, a scratchy blanket against her bare back. And late one night in the kitchen, naked and laughing when they'd realized they'd left the blinds open so anyone walking past could catch an eyeful.

Yet she couldn't ignore the overwhelming resonance of the final few months.

You can't do it, not like this.

Her eyes flew open and she jerked forward, breaking the warm contact of his lips on her neck before quickly turning to face him. She saw confusion in his eyes.

Her fingers dug into the wood door frame, holding her up and keeping her steady while everything inside groaned in abject disappointment.

"I'm sorry, Matt. I…I can't."

"What?" He frowned as his hand slowly slid from the frame. "I thought—"

"I'm sorry," she repeated lamely.

No! No, no, no. Her hands tightened on the door, breath caught in sudden hesitancy. He was right there in front of her, her memories a pale comparison to the reality of his warm body, skilled lips and practiced hands.

No. This wasn't right.

It took all her willpower to steel herself against those seductive eyes and take a firm step past him, into the hall. "I can't do this. I'm… Goodbye, Matthew."

Then she turned on her heel and practically sprinted to the elevators.

Four

It was Thursday, surgery roster day. It was always odd walking the halls of Saint Catherine's as a visitor and not rushing on his way to surgery, post-op or a meeting. Matt had passed reception and greeted the nurses, their unspoken questions creating a tiny frisson of discomfort as they returned his smile and nodded. The corridors held that familiar polarizing smell—people either loathed the mix of antiseptic, antibiotics and clean linen or found it comforting. For him it was about adrenaline, the scent of new scrubs, the weird soapy smell in the washroom. The jitters that always hit him a second after he gowned up. Then the rush of complete and utter calm as he scrubbed, studied his notes and prepared to cut.

He automatically glanced at the door numbers, then turned his focus down the hall. Katrina's office was at the end and, as always, he had to go past the Blue Room to get there.

He picked up the pace, studiously ignoring the innocuous door with its private sign. He'd always hated that room: a room where bad news got officially delivered, where parents learned their child's illness was terminal, where brothers, sisters, husbands and wives broke down and cried. The other surgeons called it "the grief room" in private.

A room he associated with so many names—Kyle McClain. Denise Baxter. Eli Hughes. Valerie Bowman. And the rest. He remembered them all.

Head cloudy with memories, he barely heard his name

being called until he spotted a middle-aged couple heading down a corridor on his left.

"Dr. Cooper?" the woman said again, and he paused as they approached. "I thought it was you. It's Megan Ross," she added with a smile. "This is Jeremy. I don't know if you remember us—"

"Of course," he said, shaking Jeremy Ross's hand. "I operated on your son, Scott." Matt paused, then asked cautiously, "Is he okay?"

"He's perfect." Scott's father waved away his concern with a reassuring smile. "We're just visiting a friend."

He nodded, relieved. "Good. Scott would be what—fourteen now? Oh, okay—" He paused as Megan Ross enveloped him in a huge hug.

"I'm sorry," she apologized, face flushed as she let him go. "But it's the least we can do for the man who saved Scotty's life."

He smiled. "That was my job, Mrs. Ross."

"Oh, no, you did more than that. You walked us through the procedure, answered all our questions and reassured us we were doing the right thing." Her voice wavered and she gulped in a breath, giving her husband a shaky smile when he reached out to rub her back. "You gave up your time, sitting with us, talking about silly, inconsequential things and keeping us occupied while we waited for Scotty to come out of post-op. We were here for a month and you were there for us every time. Not many doctors would do that."

Matt's heart squeezed for one moment, remembering the little boy with the brain tumor, one of his very last cases at Saint Cat's. "You are quite welcome."

"We've just come back from Greece, went to all those places you told us about that night," Jeremy Ross added. "Scotty loved it." He stuck his hand in his pocket and withdrew a small drawstring bag. "We got you something."

He put up a hand, alarmed. "Oh, you didn't have to—"

"Don't you go refusing it," Mrs. Ross chided. "Scott picked it out especially for you."

Could he feel any more awkward? Yet as the parents beamed at him with gratitude, the feeling fragmented. He took the velvet bag Mr. Ross held out and tipped the contents onto his palm.

"It's Saint Luke," Mrs. Ross said. "Patron Saint of Physicians. We got it on Naxos. They make them from the crumbling stones of the Gateway to the Gods."

"It's beautiful," he said, turning the cool stone figurine over in his fingers. Intricate carvings detailed the ancient saint's intricately folded robe and beard. He had a beatific expression on his lined face and he held a thick book in his hand.

A wave of emotion hit the back of Matt's throat. "Tell Scotty it's perfect."

"We will. You know he wants to be a doctor when he grows up?"

He nodded. "He'll make a good one."

After another hug and handshake, they left. And Matt was left standing there in the cool corridor, completely undone.

He remembered everything so clearly, every moment he'd spent in their company, deflecting their grief and uncertainty with hard facts, then with uncomplicated amusing stories of his sister's travels. They were good people, easy to talk to and relax around. Eventually conversation had turned to his own hopes, his plans to travel and see the world—plans that were merely a pipe dream considering his insane workload and commitment to the hospital. And the Rosses had regaled him with their ten-year-old's antics, his love of science and classic *Doctor Who* episodes, his obsession with all things ancient.

Had it really been four years ago? The desire had been planted then, only months before his brother Jack's death, before his life had taken a one-eighty and he'd turned his back on his parents' demands, his career and his marriage.

Matt dragged a hand through his hair and stared down the long corridor. He'd finally seen the world, been to places he'd desperately wanted to go. He'd spent a whole year doing nothing except experiencing life. These days, GEM ensured his travel bug was sufficiently fed: he handpicked his assignments and delegated the rest to his capable staff.

He'd achieved all his goals. Well, except one. One deep desire that burned in the back of his mind, one so powerful that it had contributed to his marriage's downfall, turned Katrina so bitter and angry that she'd demanded way more in the divorce than she was legally entitled to. Wracked with guilt, he'd given it to her.

I don't want kids. She'd made that clear from the very start. And he'd agreed. He'd witnessed the devastation of losing a child, seen the agony and pain every day. You couldn't escape it in a place like this. Plus, where would they find the time to devote to parenthood? Their entire lives revolved around equally demanding careers.

Then Jack had died and life as he knew it came crashing to a halt.

No, Katrina had said calmly when he'd broached the subject. *I told you. We agreed.*

I know, he'd replied, unable to meet her accusing eyes. *But I've changed my mind.*

She'd sighed. *Look, we should take a break. I'll get Kylie to book us a holiday.... We could spend a few days in Bali—*

I don't want a holiday, he'd shot back. *I want you to consider us having a baby.*

Oh, the look he'd gotten from that! And when she'd slowly crossed her arms in that I'm-tired-of-this-topic way of hers, he knew before she opened her mouth that his marriage was over.

That will never, ever happen, Matthew.

His phone beeped, breaking into his thoughts. He glanced at it. He was five minutes late. Katrina hated tardiness.

With a sigh, he approached the conference room door and knocked, then walked straight on in.

Five

"I'm sorry…do you have another meeting, Matthew?"

Matt glanced up from his watch to meet Katrina's cool gaze before leaning back in his seat and crossing his ankles beneath the conference table. "No."

Suddenly Matt and his ex-wife were the sole focus of attention in the room as the department heads' soft chatter came to a halt. Matthew remained impassive in the silence. Sure, for most of the staff his history with Katrina was a nonissue, but there were a few who gleefully anticipated a domestic incident every time they assembled to discuss his company's staffing needs, which Saint Cat's played a large part in fulfilling.

They obviously didn't know her. Or him. Their divorce had been polite, dispassionate and completely professional—just like their marriage.

He cocked one eyebrow up, inviting her to press the issue. She blinked a slow and icy dismissal before continuing with the agenda.

He furtively eyed his watch again. Half past one. Jeez, he hated these meetings. Every year admin rehashed the same concerns about working with GEM—low staff numbers, budgetary constraints, rostering conflicts—before finally signing on the dotted line. So as Katrina's people squabbled over the same issues, he stared out the window and let his thoughts drift back to AJ.

Five days had passed. Five days of meetings, flights and a hundred other professional commitments that had succeeded in keeping his mind firmly on work. Not on a certain redhead who'd invaded his downtime and strengthened his interest despite her unceremonious rejection.

He shifted in his chair and crossed his arms, his gaze going to the stunning view of Sydney Harbour out the window of the twentieth-floor conference room.

Man, he'd been right, though. AJ *had* changed. She'd gone from a spontaneous free spirit to…what? She'd never talked about her dreams, her wants. Never even mentioned family. Until the wedding he'd had no idea she had a sister. Yet they'd been together six months. Surely they'd talked, right?

What he knew about her could fit on the head of a pin. Prior to working at the local café near his Central Coast house, she'd traveled up and down Australia from northern Queensland to Victoria, doing seasonal fruit picking, waitressing and cleaning. Her nomadic existence fascinated him, given all his plans and constant schedules.

He remembered calling her on his last shift and, no matter what the time, she'd be on his doorstep when he got home. They'd end up in bed, then eat, make love some more, and in the morning she'd be gone. And then there was the way he'd handled their breakup, which was, he admitted, sudden and with little finesse.

No wonder she shut you down.

When the meeting broke up ten minutes later, Matt sighed in relief and headed straight out the door, checking his phone messages as he went. Delete. Delete. Answer. Ignore.

He stopped abruptly, staring at the screen.

AJ was at GEM. He checked the time of his office manager's text, then his watch. She'd been waiting in his office for two hours.

"Now that's interesting," he murmured.

A burst of anticipation quickened his blood, and he frowned. *Forget it. You took a cold shower, spent the rest of the day in a black mood then moved on.*

Apparently not.

* * *

He'd barely got a handle on his curiosity when he pushed through his office door at GEM's Mascot headquarters half an hour later.

He paused, noting her small start before she swiveled in her seat and looked up at him with wide blue eyes. Tellingly, she'd chosen the rigid-backed visitor's chair next to his desk instead of the comfy sofa flanking the far wall.

"Hi, Matt."

He let silence do the talking as he cataloged her appearance, from the worn blue denims, plain white V-neck T-shirt and oversized worn navy jacket to that red hair tightly contained in a low knot.

Man, that was beginning to piss him off.

"What brings you to Sydney?" he finally asked.

"You." She paused, a small frown marring her forehead. "Can you sit? I need to talk to you."

He shrugged and walked over to his desk, lowering himself slowly into the plush leather seat.

Was she here for a do-over?

Pride nipped at his heels, making him frown. He had half a mind to ask her to leave, but at the last moment decided against it. No harm in letting her talk, right? He could always say no.

He remained expressionless as he eyeballed her. She returned his stare.

Damn it, he *wanted* to say no.

Yeah, who're you kidding? If she *was* here to have another go of it, he'd make her stew a little. Then they'd do it his way.

His, imagination went into overdrive as he considered the endless possibilities. He'd take down that ridiculous hairdo for a start. And have her wear something…red. Yeah. A strapless body-hugging red dress that emphasized her delicate collarbone, with those crazy curls falling over her shoulders. And beneath the dress—

"Matt?"

"Yeah?" Her sharp tone snapped his attention back to the

present. When he finally looked at her—really looked—her serious expression set off all kinds of alarms. "What's going on?"

"I need your help with something."

AJ chose her words carefully, instinctively moving to cross her arms before she realized what she was doing. She linked her fingers together in her lap instead.

No, that wasn't right, either. So she recrossed her legs and slid her elbows onto the chair arms, her fingers lightly gripping the ends. Much better.

Her brief composure dissolved under the weight of Matthew's loaded question. "My help?"

"Yes. Well, it's more like a favor. Well, not a favor, which sounds a little trivial, but more like—"

"Take a breath." His smooth, cultured voice flowed over her, bringing the nervousness down a notch. "You flew down to Sydney to ask me for a favor?"

"Yes."

"What's wrong with the phone?"

"This isn't a phone kind of favor."

His mouth suddenly tweaked. "I think I know what this is about."

She blinked. "You do?"

"Yeah. But you used to come right out and say it, AJ. Hesitancy wasn't one of your attributes."

What? She shook her head with a frown. "I'm not entirely—"

"—convinced we should do it?" He leaned forward, planting his elbows on the desk and clasping his hands, an expectant gleam in his eyes. "Wouldn't denial be worse?"

AJ opened her mouth but nothing came out. This was so not going the way she'd planned. Instead of calmly presenting her situation, then laying out the solution in a businesslike manner, she'd let him stall her with one quirk of his sensual lips. Not to mention the heated stare, which melted her senses and sent her body into an anticipatory tingle.

It was déjà vu, except now they were in his office instead of the Palazzo Versace's private cabana. And just like before, that evil little voice echoed: *you have him ready to go—you don't actually have to tell him.*

Yet through the growing tangle of desire another more powerful emotion grabbed hold. Honesty. It's what had stopped her the first time. It's what would always stop her.

"Matthew. I…uh…." She hesitated, casting her eyes over his desk. There was a small mountain of files, a laptop, phone, coffee cup, scattered pens and paper. No family photos, no personal mementoes. The wall behind him held his various diplomas, a crazy-looking yearly schedule, medical diagrams and charts; it was the office of someone who'd had a life plan since he was ten years old. He was Matthew Cooper, work-driven, goal-oriented. He had been—and always would be—a career guy. Ten years later that was still blindingly obvious.

That realization bolstered her courage. "I want a baby."

His sharp inward breath was harsh in the sudden silence and she paused. If ever there was a moment-killer, this was it.

"What?" he choked out.

"I…" She pressed her lips together, working hard to contain the swelling emotion. A few seconds passed, then a few more before she finally got a handle on it. "I'm thirty-two and single. I've met guys but none who—" She swallowed and looked Matt straight in the eye. "I don't want marriage or a husband—just a baby. I've done my homework, even went to a fertility clinic, but my time is running out and it's so expensive and things fell through and—"

"And you want me to recommend a doctor for you?"

"No. I want you to be the donor."

He shot to his feet so fast it made her gasp. She stood, too, even as the ferocity of his expression had her inwardly cringing. "I did have someone lined up," she forged on. "But he—"

"Who?"

"Just some guy. A donor—"

"You thought I was more convenient than 'just some guy'?"

She winced. "That's not what I mean. I've been thinking—"

"Have you?" His lip curled, nostrils flaring. "Since when?"

"Since you called me the morning after Emily's wedding."

He said nothing, just put his hands on his hips and fixed her with such a furious glare that it felt like her face was on fire. "Look, Matt, I know your job is your life. You've invested everything in your career—it's what you live and breathe every day. I totally get that. Don't you see this is a perfect arrangement for us both? I'm not asking you to give anything up because I plan on raising this child by myself."

She paused deliberately, putting on a brave show of outward calm while her insides hammered away like a windup toy. At his narrow-eyed silence, she pressed her point. "This isn't a plan to trap you into marriage or demand child support, and I'll sign anything you want to convince you of that. This would just be a simple…exchange. It wouldn't disrupt your life. Once I'm pregnant, we'd go our separate ways."

She was met with silence.

He crossed his arms, his expression cold. "You have *got* to be kidding."

She bit her bottom lip. "Can we talk about this? I thought—"

"No." He shook his head curtly. "This isn't a favor, AJ. It's a goddamn lifelong decision!"

"For me, yes. Not for you."

His eyes raked her with such ferocity that she nearly flinched. "I was right. You have changed."

Her bravado crumpled but she refused to let the hurt show. "What makes you so righteous? You don't know what my life's been like, Matt."

"No, I don't. I never did, remember? We were just in it for a good time."

Another cheap shot. "Can you tell me what you have to lose? I'm not asking for a piece of your life. I don't expect a relationship or marriage or anything except—"

"Except sex?"

"Yes." She tipped her chin up. "We've done no-strings-attached sex before. Why not now?"

He said nothing as he stood there, hands back on hips, his mouth an angry slash. AJ met his fierce look with one of her own.

Finally, he glanced down at his watch. "I'm due in a meeting in twenty minutes. Sue at the front desk can arrange a cab for you."

"But—"

He cut her off by striding to the door and swinging it wide-open. His expression had all the hallmarks of battered pride combined with tightly wound impatience.

She'd insulted him and now he wanted her gone.

With a dry swallow she cleared her throat, refusing to let the bitter disappointment take the form of tears.

"If you change your mind…" She started then snapped her mouth shut when he fixed her with a chilly glare. She tried not to let that affect her as she straightened her shoulders and walked out the door. It was only when she strode down the corridor and retreated to the cool privacy of the bathroom that everything inside her collapsed.

She leaned against the closed stall door, choking back her abject disappointment. *It's not the end. You still have the clinic.* And Emily would help her, as much as she loathed asking for money. She'd just have to swallow her pride and her tightly held beliefs and ask.

Yeah, she really was Charlene's daughter, wasn't she? Begging for money, expecting a handout. The only difference was she'd honor her debt, not do a runner in the middle of the night to avoid it.

The bitter irony of it all made her heart ache.

Six

Matt paced his office, swinging from outrage to indignation then back again. He paused at the wall, did an about turn then continued pacing.

Damn room was way too small. He scrubbed at his chin, then his cheek, before running a hand into his hair.

What the hell had just happened?

He was insulted. No, more than that—he was deeply offended. Did she really think he was that kind of guy? He snorted, hands on his hips. These past few days all made sense now: AJ's initial coldness, then suddenly agreeing to his invitation. She wanted a convenient stud. Not *him*—just what he could give her.

His hands curled into fists as fury overcame him.

And yet…

He must be the worst kind of idiot, letting his need lead him around like a dog on a leash because he *still* wanted her. Un-fricking-believable.

He stopped and glared out the window, studying the slow ascent of a Qantas jumbo jet as it climbed into the sky. So she thought he was some kind of mindless workaholic man whore, did she? That he'd jump at her offer then happily walk away when she'd gotten what she wanted?

With a curse, he collapsed into his chair, the leather protesting under the sudden weight. AJ Reynolds was trouble. Not worth the stress. Hell, he could pick up the phone and choose from a handful of willing women for an uncomplicated lay.

Since his divorce it was all he'd been prepared to give. GEM occupied his every waking moment; he'd deliberately made it that way so there'd be no room to dwell on the bitter disappointment of Katrina's rejection.

Yet something stirred inside, reminding him of his deeply buried dreams.

Dragging a hand over his chin, he tapped one finger on his bottom lip.

"Why me?" he muttered, his gaze skimming the blue skyline until it latched on to another plane in the distance. Surely there were dozens of eager guys queuing up for the pleasure. Yet when he tried to picture AJ with another man, doing all those things they'd done, touching her, making love to her, something nasty and painful twisted in his gut.

No.

A firm knock startled him from his reverie and he turned to see a familiar figure in the doorway. "Matt? Got a minute?"

"Sure." He straightened his shoulders and nodded.

"Really?" His head of security, James Decker, tipped his chin down and peered over the rims of his dark aviator sunglasses. "Because it looks like you're thinking hard about something important."

Matt sighed. "I've had an offer. And I'm not sure I should take it."

Decker stepped inside the office, closing the door behind him. As always, he was dressed in black—muscle T-shirt, army pants, boots and gun belt. Matt often teased Deck about his militant vigilante look, and the head of security would always come back with, "At least I save your ass." The black was for show, for his team to project power and confidence to the public. It often meant the difference between success and failure when faced with life-threatening situations.

"What's the offer?" Decker asked, crossing his arms over his broad chest.

"A woman, no relationship strings attached."

Decker's whistle came out low. "Lucky bastard. A hot woman?"

"Oh, yeah."

"And your problem is?"

"She's...an old flame."

Decker's hands went to his hips. "Crazy chick, then?"

"God, no. She's—" Matt paused, his mouth curving in remembrance. "AJ's perfectly sane."

"AJ?" Decker's brow dipped. "Not *the* AJ?"

Crap. He'd wondered when that night would come back to bite him in the ass. A close call in Mexico, the hotel bar, expensive whiskey... He and Deck had gotten comfortably drunk and ended up comparing a handful of regrets.

"I take it from your silence it's the same girl," Decker said, his look knowing. "And you want strings."

Matt grabbed the nearest paper and glared at it, feeling his neck flush. "Forget I said anything, okay?"

"Dude, this is me you're talking to here." Decker grabbed a chair, straddled it and crossed his arms over the back. "I've saved your life a dozen times. We've been in the middle of Vietnam, ass-deep in mud. We've run from Zimbabwean vigilantes, dodged bullets in East Timor." He grinned. "And I wasn't that drunk. I remember everything you said."

Matt sighed. Decker was six feet of contained Yankee firepower, all cocky American attitude and muscle with a huge gun fetish. He also happened to be his best mate, not to mention one of the most brilliant strategists he'd ever met.

"She wants more than just sex," Matt said.

"Marriage?"

"No. A baby." Despite the seriousness of the conversation, Decker's curse made Matt grin. "I knew that'd get you."

"She straight up said she wants you to father her kid?"

"Yep."

"What's the catch?"

"Nothing. I get her pregnant, then I can walk away."

Decker snorted. "Like that's gonna happen." He looked

Matt over. "So tell her no. Unless…" His eyes turned shrewd. "You *want* a kid. With her."

That was the question, wasn't it? Did he want a baby with AJ?

Deck and he had shared some moments, but he'd never told anyone this. It meant he'd have to admit that the complicated wound of losing his brother and Katrina's rejection was still fresh in his mind, even four years on.

"I'll take that as a yes," Decker said.

Yeah, the guy wasn't dumb. Not by a long shot.

Decker drummed his fingers on the back of the chair. "Is it possible she's lying to trap you?"

Matt grunted. "Nope. She was painfully clear she just wants a donor."

"Huh."

"What's that supposed to mean?"

"You still have a thing for her."

Matt's frown deepened. "What makes you say that?"

Decker shrugged. "A, because of what you told me all those years ago, and B, because we're still talking about it. You've never put this much thought into a woman before."

"So I have a problem."

"Not really. Dude, you live for a challenge. We wouldn't have half our clients without your Mister Charm-and-Persuasion routine. And do I need to list all the women who've succumbed to your moody charm?" He ticked them off on his fingers. "Snooty French heiress. Billionaire ice queen. Italian model…"

"AJ's different," Matt interrupted.

"I'm getting that loud and clear. Are you?" Decker gave him a meaningful look. "There's obviously something still there. You won't know if you don't make an effort."

"Yeah, but—"

"I'm just saying that if anyone can convince a woman to fall in love with them, it's you. Who wouldn't want the great and powerful Matthew Cooper?" He grinned and stood. "You know the drill—background, assessment, decision, follow-through. I'll come back later and we can talk about our Italian job."

Long after Decker had left Matt stared at the closed door.

Background. Assessment. Decision. Follow-through. "BADFIT" was GEM's standard operating procedure when deciding to take on a new client. Yet this was AJ they were talking about, not another job. It wasn't designed for this kind of situation.

Didn't mean it wouldn't work.

There was only one way to find out.

He reached for the phone and dialed.

"Final call for Flight DJ 512 to the Gold Coast. Would all passengers for Flight DJ 512 please make their way to gate twenty-seven as your plane is now ready for takeoff."

AJ rushed off the moving walkway, readjusted the satchel strap across her shoulders, then broke into a jog, wheeling her suitcase behind her. Her sneakers squeaked on the polished floor as the Sydney terminal windows flashed by. Twenty-four, twenty-five…

Twenty-seven. She ground to a halt, shoving back a loose curl from her ponytail. The line was still a dozen people deep.

With a relieved sigh, she dug in her bag and grabbed the boarding pass. The cheap ticket was nonrefundable and she wasn't about to impose on her brother-in-law's generosity and squat another night in his newly built Potts Point apartment, not when he had potential buyers waiting in the wings.

Just then her phone rang, and after three rings she finally found it at the bottom of her bag.

It was Matthew. She shuffled forward in the line. "Yes?"

"Where are you?"

She frowned, eyeing the moving queue. "Why?"

"We need to talk."

"Please remember all phones must be turned off," the flight attendant politely announced, her gaze lingering on AJ as she reached out for her boarding pass. AJ shook her head and stepped out of line, allowing a man in a business suit to grumble past.

She fiddled with her bag strap. "Look, I'm just about to get on a plane. If you want to yell at me again—"

"I just want to talk about your...proposal."

"Ma'am? Are you boarding?" The flight attendant's respectful smile flickered with impatience.

"AJ?" Matt said in her ear.

AJ wavered as she eyed the cavernous departure tunnel that would take her back to her life. A vaguely unsatisfying life, one that lacked true purpose and follow-through after she'd finally decided what she wanted.

"What do you want to say?" she finally asked.

She heard him sigh. "Can we not do this over the phone?"

"My flight is boarding, Matt. Unless you have a spare ticket to compensate me for my fare—"

"Done. I'll pick you up downstairs in twenty minutes."

"But—"

"You wanted to talk. So we'll talk."

She sighed. That didn't mean he'd say anything she wanted to hear. She wasn't about to get her hopes up to have him crush them all over again: she'd done that once and look where that had gotten her.

"You still there?"

"Yes." She rubbed at the spot behind her ear, tugging on the lobe.

"AJ, you're asking for my help. I need to know details before I commit either way."

"Miss," the flight attendant said, her smile tight. "I'll need to have your boarding pass."

That's when AJ finally made a choice. "Okay," she said into the phone, numbly shaking her head at the attendant and turning away. "Twenty minutes."

Seven

AJ waited in the pickup bay, hesitant anticipation congealing in her stomach. The longer she stood there, the tighter her nerves got. Did this mean he'd changed his mind about her proposal? Surely it did. He wouldn't make her miss her flight just to tell her what a dumb idea it was, right?

Still, it didn't stop her from nervously humming *The Wizard of Oz* theme song under her breath. "Somewhere Over the Rainbow"—a familiar soothing song she used to sing to Emily when they were kids, drowning out their parents on a drunken bender, partying loudly at two in the morning. While strangers passed out in the bathroom or stormed up and down the hall, Emily had crawled into AJ's bed and they'd held each other in the scary dark. And AJ had waveringly sung that song about hopes and dreams and following them to find a better place.

Don't think about them. Think about yourself, about what's happening right here, right now.

By the time she spotted the sleek ash-gray Jaguar purring up to the parking bay, she'd worked herself into a state. Yet she still noticed a dozen pairs of eyes swivel to take in the sporty car, their gaze running over the smooth lines with a mix of envy, joy and blatant lust.

Then Matt eased from the driver's seat and she could swear she heard the appreciative murmurs, even over the general chaos of Sydney airport.

He was dressed for serious business—dark gray suit, white shirt, green tie, mirrored sunglasses. He wore the clothes on his lean frame with such casual elegance, a commanding uniform that befitted the CEO of a national corporation. Then he pushed up his glasses and rounded the car in a few strides, leaning down to grab her carry-on. But when his hand went to her shoulder, she instinctively stepped back.

He frowned. "Can I take your bag?"

Embarrassment made her flush. "Oh, yeah. Sure."

He gently eased the strap down, his knuckles grazing her arm, and she barely had time to get flustered before he was hoisting it over his shoulder, then turning to open the passenger door.

She took the opportunity to note the way his jacket tightened across his back when he leaned in to deposit her bags in the tiny backseat. The touchable skin where collar met neck. And the firm way those long-fingered hands grasped the door as he motioned for her to get in.

AJ took a breath and did just that.

It wasn't often she got to revel in the luxury of a sleek European car. Zac guarded his Porsche like the thing was made of eighteen-carat gold, and her bomby Getz was hardly in the same league. But this…this was heaven: soft suede seats cupping her bottom, the distinct smell of money, new car and leather permeating the air. She sat low, way too low, and the sensation was an odd mix of indulgence and discomfort.

"Since when do you have a Jag?" she asked as he buckled up.

"I got it last year." She barely heard the engine kick in before he glanced over his shoulder, turned the steering wheel and merged into traffic while the radio played softly through the speakers. "The Sultan of El-Jahir was very generous."

She blinked. "El-Jahir? Where's that?"

"Tiny independent island off the coast of Africa. The palace guards staged a coup and GEM treated the Sultan's third wife after a hostage drama."

"And he gave you a Jag."

"He originally offered one of his daughters."

AJ snorted out a laugh. "And you turned him down?"

"I'm not the arranged-marriage type."

Their moment of levity lapsed into elongated silence as they made their way out onto Qantas Drive.

"So you said you wanted to talk," she finally said.

His eyes remained on the road. "Out of all the men you know, why me?"

Her mouth thinned. "All the men I know? How many do you think I *know*, Matt?"

His startled gaze met hers. "I didn't mean it that way. I..." He returned his attention to the road and frowned. "You *were* a free spirit—impulsive, crazy. Up for anything. And," he added when she opened her mouth, "I was the one with the rules and the life plan. I'd always figured you'd end up with a guy more on your wavelength." He flicked her a brief glance. "You didn't meet someone else after me?"

"I met a few someone elses. You didn't ruin me for every other man, if that's what you're implying."

"Good to know."

"You don't sound glad."

"I am." The car purred along the road, dashing past the huge Etihad Airlines billboard and DHL's avant garde cube sculpture. "Me, I got married."

"Yeah, so you said. Let me guess..." She paused, taking the moment to study his profile, unashamedly lingering on the aquiline nose and full lips. "A church wedding with lots of influential colleagues on the guest list. The reception was probably at some swanky Sydney restaurant—Rockpool. Maybe Luke Mangan's place at the Hilton. The bride's dress would've been sleek and classic, something subdued but gorgeously elegant. A society queen—no," AJ amended, "another doctor, someone beautiful and ambitious and parent-approved."

Matt said nothing, the Jaguar purring softly in the silence as they drove.

"Am I right?" AJ probed.

He shrugged. "Pretty much."

Despite everything, the confirmation still stung. Huh. *She'd* never been parent-approved.

She thought back to a night she'd rather forget, a moment when she'd gone against every survival instinct, every ingrained memory from her fractured past and put herself out there, only to have her hopes destroyed seconds later.

She crossed her arms, pushing back into the leather seat. She had to focus on the here and now, not dwell on the past. It was how she survived, how she'd always survived.

"So why do you want a baby?" Matt asked.

A million reasons that she didn't have the time or inclination to discuss because that would mean talking about her past and her emotions. And those two things were off-limits. Instead, she settled on the most urgent one. "Because there's a possibility I can't. Three months ago I had surgery for ovarian cysts and they found extensive scarring. Apparently, I have a less than a thirty percent chance of conceiving."

His brief glance spoke volumes yet revealed nothing. "Why me?"

She turned, giving him her full attention. "Why not you? We know each other, and we're sexually compatible. I won't make any emotional or financial demands. You not only get no-strings-attached sex, but you also won't have the hassle of a baby. Life will go on as normal." She shrugged. "We both win."

What the hell could Matt say to that?

She wanted him to make a baby. Only she didn't want him around afterward. The situation was laughable except he'd never felt like laughing less in his entire life.

He made a quick left turn and they pulled into a side street. After he cranked on the handbrake and cut the engine, he turned to face her.

"Well?" she said, arching her eyebrows. She looked confident, her hands clasped in her lap, her head tilted just so, a firm, almost fierce look in her eyes. He remembered that look. He'd missed it.

He'd missed her.

His gut bottomed out. After all these years, after every turn his life had taken, how could that be? But the truth sat right there in his passenger seat, her flame-red hair pulled back in an efficient ponytail, her lean body inadvertently emphasized by jeans and a fitted T.

She'd made it clear what she wanted, and it didn't include him.

He'd worked hard to get where he was. Whenever he decided to pursue a goal, he committed everything to it. He hated the failure that his divorce had wrought, hated that Katrina had not only ridiculed his suggestion that they start a family but also had refused point-blank to even consider it. And now here was AJ, a ghost from his past, offering up his deepest desire. After Katrina's refusal he'd managed to bury those feelings deep, focusing instead on forging a new career from the tattered remnants.

The irony was that AJ had no idea. She still thought he was some career-driven workaholic robot, motivated by success and money. Yet he was no longer the man she knew from back then, that young, overscheduled, goal-oriented man for whom career and the great Cooper name came first and foremost.

Decker was right. Everything he'd pursued he'd gotten— his position as chief surgeon at Saint Cat's, GEM, various bed partners following Katrina. As a doctor, he'd been acutely aware of human frailty, the crazy ways a person's life could hinge on the actions of others. Yet he was also a big believer in fate. He'd never been able to replicate the magic he'd had with AJ, not even with Katrina. But now, incredibly, he was being handed a second chance.

Fate.

Was he crazy? Maybe. But right now, he had the eerie feeling that if he said no to AJ, if he didn't put in the effort to make another go of it, he'd lose her and she'd have their happy ending with someone else.

You're actually going to make a woman fall in love with

you? He could imagine Paige's incredulity just before she burst out laughing.

This was no laughing matter. He had no intention of walking away—didn't want to walk away. AJ had chosen *him,* had come to him.

Fate.

He eyeballed her as she waited patiently for his answer.

"So there's been no one else?"

AJ slowly slid her sunglasses off, placed them high on her head, then met his direct look with one of her own. "One guy loved going out with his mates more than me. One preferred his collection of *Lord of the Rings* action figures. Another had three girls on the go. And one…" She paused. Those battle scars still stung—no doubt would still sting—for years to come. But their presence also proved she was doing the right thing.

"What happened?"

"He came close." She shrugged. No naïveté for her again. "But then I found out he was married and cheating on his wife." At his gently murmured curse she shrugged. "See? Asshats."

"You're still young, AJ. Only thirty-two. There's still plenty of time to—"

"God help me, if you say, 'you'll find someone,' I am so going to smack you."

He clamped his mouth shut and stared out the windshield, the faint strains of traffic barely discernible in the background. "So you've decided to approach motherhood alone," he said.

"Yes."

He paused, eyebrow raised, waiting for her to elaborate.

She sighed and gripped the seat belt still strapped across her chest. "Given my single status and my low chances of getting pregnant, I'd booked an appointment with a fertility clinic, but that fell through and I have to wait six months for another."

"Which is where I come in."

"Yes. Matt, look. Maybe it was just a coincidence seeing you at Emily's wedding. I'm not a believer in fate—"

"I am."

She paused, digesting that interesting little snippet, then continued. "So if you want me to sign a contract, I will. I will not interfere with your life or your career. No one will have to know."

"Keep us a secret?" His brow went up. "You didn't like that idea last time."

"You remember that?"

"You don't?"

Every single moment I think of you. She swallowed the faint feeling of inadequacy, still there after all these years. "It was a long time ago. I'm older now. And I'm prepared to meet your terms."

He remained silent for a moment, then said softly, "You don't know what my terms are."

She suppressed a shiver as his gaze passed over her face, taking in her features before focusing squarely on her eyes. *Wait, did that mean—?*

Her heart skipped a beat. "What are they?" she asked softly.

"Well, first—you have to be able to financially support a child."

"I can." Her calm response belied the growing butterflies in her stomach.

"Because I get the impression your income could be…" He paused, searching for a word. "Fickle."

The implication stung. "Sometimes. But my bank account is decent. Do you want to check my balance?"

"No, that won't be necessary." His gaze skimmed her again. "And having Zac Prescott as financial backup wouldn't hurt, I'm guessing."

Oh, now she was more than stung. She was irritated. "Yeah, sponging off my brother-in-law is not—and never has been—an option, Matt. What's your next condition?"

"Do you have an apartment? A place of your own?"

"I'm looking."

He nodded.

"Saint Cat's fertility specialist is the best in the state. I can get an appointment for a week Thursday."

"That's quick."

His smile was brief. "The perks of being the former head of neurosurgery."

With a nod she asked, "Is that all?" then immediately hated the way her voice came out all stuttery and unsure.

"No." This time his eyes lingered on her cheek, then her lips. "We're going to do this the old-fashioned way. No clinics, no cups. It'll be just you, me and a bed. Or—" his mouth curved "—maybe not a bed. Depends where we are."

AJ's breath stilled. This was…unbelievable. Amazing.

"So you're saying yes," she said out loud. "We're really going to do this."

Matt nodded. "We are."

He'd said yes. He'd actually said *yes*. Reality struck so hard and with such force that her throat closed up and she had to work to regain control of her overwhelming emotions.

One step. This was just one step.

Yet the yearning, the desperate desire, flickered to life, flaring into hope.

A baby. Her baby. A chubby, squirmy, drooly child who would know every day he was loved and wanted. A child who would never go hungry or thirsty. A child who would always come first. A child she'd hold and cuddle and never abandon to the foster system.

She quickly suppressed those bitter memories, locking them away so they wouldn't taint the moment. "Thank you, Matt," she choked out, her hand going to his arm. "Honestly, I cannot thank you enough. This means…" She blinked like crazy and took a breath as the skeins of control began to unwind. *Don't cry. Don't you dare cry!*

"Do you want me to draw up a formal agreement?"

She stilled as reality jolted her back to awareness. "Can you do that?" At his nod she said, "Oh, okay, then. Sure."

Of course, having something down in writing made total sense. She withdrew her hand and glanced at her watch. "So I guess...well, I'm free right now. When do you want to...uh..."

His cough of surprise made her glance up. "AJ."

"Yes?"

"Let's not get ahead of ourselves. Let's see what Dr. Adams says on Thursday."

She could feel the warmth heat her cheeks.

"And anyway," he added casually, "we're going out first."

"Going out? What, on a date?"

"Yes. Tonight. You, me, dinner. Dessert."

AJ hesitated. "Although I appreciate the effort, you really don't have to do that, you know." She smiled, tempering her refusal. "At this stage, it's safe to say I'm a sure thing."

"But I want to. Big difference."

She met his eyes, holding firm under his loaded gaze. So he was determined to wine and dine her before bedding her? AJ shrugged. "Fine," she said in her best blasé voice. "Dinner."

"Where are you staying?" Matt asked after a brief pause.

"I don't know. I'll have to make a call first." She'd handed Zac's apartment keys over to the building super. She'd have to call him, see if she could stay longer until she could work out something that didn't involve taking advantage of her brother-in-law's charity.

"You can always stay with me."

"No!" she blurted out, then added more calmly, "No, that's not necessary. I can find a cheap hotel someplace."

"In Sydney?" He raised a skeptical eyebrow. "I have a perfectly good apartment in Paddington you can use."

She frowned. Surrounded by Matt's things from his normal life? Bad idea.

"Or..." he added slowly. "There's always my house at Pretty Beach."

Oh, no. She shook her head. She needed her own space

to keep up some emotional distance. His apartment would be bad enough, but being smack in the middle of the place where they'd made love and he'd scarred her vulnerable heart ten years ago?

Not going to happen.

"The apartment sounds fine. It'd only be for one night," she added. "I've been staying at Zac's place in Potts Point."

He nodded. "You'll need it for a few months, minimum."

"A few months?"

"How long did you expect this to take, AJ?"

"Well, apparently the Reynolds women are breeders," she muttered, recalling her mother's irritating, oft-declared statement, which was always followed by a cackle and a wheeze.

With a bemused expression, he said, "We're working with reality here, not a cute homily. Thirty percent is low but not impossible." They stopped at the traffic light and he studied her intently, gauging her reaction. "We'll need to take every single opportunity to ensure you get pregnant."

That meant every possible moment having sex with Matt.

Was it bad that she was incredibly turned on right now? That she wanted nothing more than to lean across the seat, grab his tie and plant a kiss on those sensuous lips?

And just like all the times before, he read her intent as clearly as if she'd scrawled it across her face. His eyes darkened, a slow smile teasing the corner of his mouth. Then he deliberately dropped his gaze to her mouth, resting there for agonizing seconds before dragging it up to meet her eyes once more.

The interior of the car heated up by ten degrees.

The light changed and he abruptly turned back to the road. "I'll drop you off at my place now."

Hurry. "Okay."

Twenty minutes later, when he parked in front of his apartment, gathered her bags and led the way into the lobby, her anticipation took a nosedive.

He placed the bags on the slate floor, pressed the elevator

button and held out a key. "I'm on the fifteenth floor. I'll see you at seven-thirty."

Confused, she took the key, barely registering the brief contact their hands made. "But aren't you…?"

"I have to get back to work."

"Oh. Of course." She bit back her disappointment and re-adjusted the strap on her shoulder. *This is who he is, remember? The guy consumed with work. A perfect arrangement for you.*

"AJ?"

"Yes?" She glanced up, and with a swift movement, Matt looped one finger in the top of her jeans and tugged her forward.

The kiss was brief, a mere millisecond of lips on lips. AJ registered the warmth, the seductive smell of his skin and the slight hitch in his breath. A haunting reminder of what they'd once had. And a promise of more to come.

Then it was over and Matt released her, stepping back with a grin as the elevator doors pinged open. "I'll see you tonight. Wear a dress and heels."

She could only nod numbly as she watched him stride through the lobby, all male efficiency and confidence. In stark contrast, emotion churned wildly in her gut, an annoying response to his kiss.

Get a grip, AJ. Put on your big girl panties and deal with this. With a nod, she yanked her suitcase handle and strode into the elevator, Matt's apartment key firm in her clenched hand.

She would not expect anything more than what it was—a physical union to produce a baby. She'd enjoyed men before without the emotional commitment—she could do the same with Matthew Cooper.

Eight

AJ submerged herself in the huge spa bath so that only her mouth remained above the surface. The warm water lapped around her cheeks and over her eyelids, making her breath echo in her ears.

Matthew Cooper had said yes and she couldn't quite believe it.

The doubt that had plagued her for the past half hour welled up again. This wouldn't be a donation from a stranger—it was Matt. Someone she'd had a physical connection with. Someone whose DNA would form part of her child, someone who'd be reflected in the child's face as he grew up.

A constant reminder of her past.

Was she completely insane or just way too focused on the end result not to have realized that before?

No. She ran her hands through her hair, the soft sodden strands floating around her face. Neither she nor Emily looked anything like her parents. Children were not clones—they were individuals with their own unique personalities.

Though her child would most likely have her curly red hair and blue eyes.

She felt the smile curve her mouth. All hers—no one else's.

"Just concentrate on tonight," she murmured, her voice bouncing off the tiled walls. Because Matt was actually taking her out. In public. On a date.

God, how she hated that word! The last time they'd had anything resembling a date was the night he'd broken up with her. Yes, she remembered it all, even if the edges had grown fuzzy with time and other lovers. She'd ordered Thai from their favorite takeaway, dressed up the table by the pool, then splurged on some fancy lingerie and wrapped herself in a satin robe, waiting for his return.

He'd been exhausted, dark circles emphasizing those poet's eyes, brow furrowed from the pressures of his day. They'd eaten in silence while she practiced her speech over and over in her head, excitement and fear tempering her hunger.

Excitement because she'd never let someone this close before. Fear because…well, she'd never let someone this close before. Every survival instinct, every wrenching past disappointment had made its mark, scarring her subconscious and shaping her into the person she was. It was a sordid, painful minefield and she purposefully avoided that area.

Never count on anyone. Never let your guard down. Never, ever get comfortable.

Despite the walls she'd built, Matt had managed to worm his way in.

Damn right it was scary.

I've been thinking…. No, too cliché. *What do you think about me moving in?* She'd frowned into her pad thai. Too direct. She'd run through a few more, before settling on, *I've decided to stay in town a bit longer. What do you think?*

She'd smiled, taken a breath, then opened her mouth to make that scary leap off the cliff.

Matt had gotten there first.

AJ, I'm sorry, but this isn't working for me anymore.

She abruptly sat up, sloshing water over the side of the tub. She was older now, wiser, with years of experience behind her. She'd thought they had meant something, but now she knew it'd all been in her head. No way would she be that vulnerable again. Ever.

With that thought she wrapped herself in a huge white towel, turbaned her hair in another and padded out into the living room. Late-afternoon sun streamed through the huge glass doors that led out onto a wrought-iron balcony housing a sleek state-of-the art Weber barbecue and a long entertainment area with an unhindered view of Sydney's CBD, Centrepoint and the Harbour Bridge.

Like the rest of the buildings on Matt's street, the 1920s facade was expertly restored. The theme continued inside the lobby, with art deco colors and marble stairs. Even the elevator, though modern, had been designed to reflect the period.

The interior of Matt's apartment was beautiful, too, but in a clean, minimalistic way. She'd gone through every room, unashamedly poked into drawers, cupboards and shelves, yet her curiosity had been far from assuaged. The only art adorning the pale blue walls were black-and-white photographs of famous places—the Colosseum, the Great Wall of China, Stonehenge. As stunning as they were, they lacked the warmth and life of a painting. The Bondi Beach watercolor she'd done last year would bring things to life—if only it weren't at home in Surfers, along with the majority of her paints and brushes.

And her clothes.

The limits of her shoestring travel wardrobe had obviously occurred to Matt, too, because he called about it ten minutes after she finished her bath. "If you need to go shopping, the concierge can—"

"Don't worry," she replied breezily. "I've got that covered."

"Okay." But he didn't sound sure and his doubt irritated her. Didn't he trust her to choose appropriate attire? They'd never been out, so he had no idea her tastes extended to more than jeans, tiny summer dresses and X-rated lingerie.

"A dress and heels, hey?" She'd hung up and readjusted her towel, tucking it tightly under her arm before tapping on her phone's contacts list. "I'll give you a dress and heels, Matthew Cooper."

He hadn't been so excited about date since…since forever, Matt thought, changing gears as he drove across Anzac Parade.

He barely recalled the details of that afternoon: a bunch of meetings, phone calls and schedule confirmations. Decker's brief of their Italian job next Sunday. Good thing his office manager put it all in his online calendar; otherwise he'd be screwed.

Yes, for a second he'd experienced doubt but he quickly shut it down. Doubt never got him anywhere, and he wouldn't start entertaining it now. This was their second chance and he was going to pull out all the stops to show her he'd changed and that the best thing for her baby was for both of them to be in its life.

A baby. He felt the crazy grin take shape before he clenched his jaw to kill it. A 30 percent chance of conception wasn't a whole lot to work with but at least it was something.

Twenty minutes later he pulled up in front of his apartment building and yanked on the brake. Anticipation accelerated his step as he strode into the brightly lit lobby.

Then he stopped dead in his tracks.

He registered black heels, a long satiny black dress with one strap tied high on her shapely shoulder. Fiery curls tumbled down her back in thick, touchable waves and her generous mouth was coated in shiny cherry-red lipstick.

Wow.

She took a few steps forward and the slinky material rippled around her legs, revealing a smooth calf and dimpled knee. "I didn't know what you had planned so…" She raised her arms a little, a tiny sparkly clutch in her hand.

"You look amazing." He unashamedly took her in.

She smiled despite her skittering gaze. Ah, now he'd thrown her. *Good.*

"Still nervous with compliments?" He raised his brow.

"Yep."

When he extended an arm, she barely hesitated before taking it. A bewitching smell of strawberries and something floral teased his senses, and he took a deep breath. "I like your hair like that."

"I know."

He couldn't help but laugh. "Honest, too."

"I find it makes things less complicated that way."

Yeah, he remembered that about her. So what would she have to say about his subterfuge? That he planned to put everything into seducing her, into making her fall in love with him?

"So, you just had a spare evening gown hanging around in your luggage?" He drew her toward the front door, her heels clicking on the smooth tiles.

"I have a girlfriend who's a fashion buyer for David Jones."

"Handy."

"Indeed." Her lips curved again, matching his smile, and his heart did a little flip at the thought of the coming evening.

Emily stared out the window as they crawled past an unobtrusive town house, light from a subdued neon sign streaming down onto the sidewalk. "We're eating at Maxfield?"

"Yep."

"George Evans's restaurant? The guy who won last year's *Master Chef?*" They turned the next corner.

"Yep."

"And you got a table on short notice?"

"Yep."

"Are you going to say anything else other than 'yep'?"

"Yep." He gave her a wink before pulling into a spare parking spot. She waited, enjoying the view as he came around the car, opened her door and offered his hand. She took it, swung her legs out and rose fluidly.

They walked hand in hand to the restaurant, the warm intimacy sending a steady thrum of delight over her skin. How could she calmly sit and eat a meal and not succumb to the desire of ripping his clothes off when he was so very close?

She thought back to ten years ago and how she'd sensed his interest the first time he'd come striding into her coffee shop. Lucy and Maz had fallen over themselves to serve him, but he'd focused on AJ, those dark, brooding eyes somehow

detecting her lust concealed beneath her efficient barista facade. The next day he'd asked for her number. That night she'd
ended up in his bed.

Just like tonight. Excitement surged at the thought.

He squeezed her hand, smiling down at her.

"Why are we having dinner again?" she asked, letting out
a breath.

"Because I'm hungry."

"Very funny. But that's not what I meant."

"I know. And we'll get to that soon enough. But right now,
can you just enjoy the evening?"

With a small huff, AJ could do nothing but nod.

The minutes dragged by, painful, boring moments in which
they were seated, given menus and the wine list and then left
to decide.

Matt folded his menu and turned his attention to her. "So,
you have a sister."

"Emily, yes." She rearranged her cutlery, aligning it perfectly with her plate.

"Older or younger?"

"Younger."

"And your parents? Are they—?"

"Not in the picture. Ever."

When she put her elbows on the table and leaned forward,
his gaze latched on to the tiny butterfly pendant at her throat
as it swung gently, glinting in the light. "Matt, look, I'd prefer we don't talk about my past."

He brought his eyes back to her and frowned. "I'm just trying to get a conversation going here."

"I know. But those people are off-limits."

Those people? Matt's brow ratcheted up but he said nothing. *Take your time. You deal with setbacks and plan devia-
tions every day. This one is no different.*

"You and Emily are close."

He heard her small sigh before she laid her arms on the table, cupping her elbows. "Now, yes."

"And before?"

"We hadn't talked in years. But we're good now." She waved a casually dismissive hand, but the deliberateness of the gesture sent up a red flag. He stored that snippet away for future reference.

"So where did you grow up?"

"Lots of places. Look, Matt—"

"Sydney? Brisbane?"

"Perth. I don't think—"

When he leaned in he didn't miss the way she ever so slightly leaned back. "Humor me, AJ. I just want a little background."

"Why?"

"Because I really know nothing about you."

"You know enough."

"No, I don't." He focused on repositioning his wineglass in order to give her time to work out an answer without feeling the pressure of his scrutiny. "For example, where did you go to school? Did you have any pets when you were a kid? What's your favorite movie? Book?"

When he finally glanced up, she was staring at him so hard, it almost felt like a rebuke. Yet he held firm and finally she said, "I stopped counting schools after six. We couldn't afford to feed ourselves, let alone any pets. I must've seen *The Wizard of Oz* a hundred times. And my favorite book? *The Magic Faraway Tree*."

"Enid Blyton?"

She nodded. "I always wanted a tree like that."

"Didn't every kid?" He smiled.

AJ remained grim. "No, I *really* wanted one."

Before he could reply, a waitress appeared. "Are you ready to order?"

He clamped his mouth shut and gave the waitress a neutral smile.

They ordered. When they were alone again, silence reigned. Matt watched the way AJ's gaze dropped, her eyelashes fanning down over her cheeks. She tucked her hands under the table and leaned forward, forearms pressed against the table edge. She still didn't meet his eyes, instead focusing solely on the fractured light streaming through the blue glass water bottle centered on their table.

"So." He poured a glass of water. "You're an artist."

She glanced up. "You could say that."

"People buy your stuff, right? So I'd say that makes you one." He pointed to her glass, and she nodded. They both watched him pour, the awkward tension punctuated only by the soft glug of water filling the glass. "What medium do you work in?"

"I don't mind oils but much prefer watercolors." She wrapped her fingers around her glass and pulled it across the table. "They dry quicker and the customers don't have to wait long."

"Did you study art at uni?"

"No. All self-taught." She took a sip of water. "Story of my life, really."

He was ready with a dozen more questions but he clamped his mouth shut instead.

A few more moments passed, moments in which she refused wine, then casually cast her eye around the restaurant, observing the diners, the staff, the decor. And he, in turn, took his time and studied her with leisurely pleasure. The curve of her cheek that he knew was just as soft as when he'd first touched it. The delicate earlobe full of sensitive nerves that made her alternately shiver then gasp. The stunning hair that curled around his fingers with a life of its own.

When her gaze finally returned to him, his expression must have given him away.

"What?"

He couldn't help but smile. "Nothing."

"Tell me," she persisted, a cautious, curious smile matching his. So he crooked his finger, beckoning her closer.

"Ten years has made you more beautiful." Startled, she pulled back, looking down at the table. "Angel, are you blushing?"

"I don't blush."

"I think you are."

She snapped her gaze back to his, eyes sparkling. "Fine. I am."

"I never knew a woman to take such offense at being called beautiful."

"Oh? So you're free and easy with your compliments, are you?"

"Women like compliments."

"I'm sure they do," she replied archly.

He grinned. "But you are…unique."

"Thanks. I think."

"You're welcome, Angel."

He heard her tiny intake of breath. "Can you stop calling me that?"

"Why? You liked it once."

She tightened her grip on the glass and glared for a few seconds. Then she shrugged and took another sip of water. "Fine, whatever."

Oh, he was getting to her, all right.

"Matt," she started casually, steadily focused on rotating her wineglass by the stem.

"Yes?"

She paused, then shook her head. "It's none of my business."

Matt leaned in. "I'll tell you if that's the case. Ask me anyway."

Her shoulders straightened, then she gave a little head tilt. "Why did you quit Saint Cat's?"

He cupped his glass in his hand, swirling the contents. "Jack—my younger brother—died four years ago."

Her gaze softened as she looked into his eyes. "Oh, Matt, I'm—"

"It's okay." He raised a hand, shaking his head. "It's fine."

It wasn't. It never would be. But she didn't need to know that.

"What happened?"

"He fell while climbing the Taurus mountain ranges in Istanbul. If emergency response had been quicker, he probably would've made it."

"Is that why you set up GEM?"

"After I dropped off the grid for a year, yeah."

"Where'd you go?"

"Nepal. China. Europe." He automatically slid the butter tray across the table as she broke her roll apart.

"How'd your parents take it?"

"Like I'd committed professional suicide."

That year consisted of a bunch of strung-together blurry memories, not much more. He'd experienced a life other than his perfectly mapped out one, drifting around on a whim, helping where he could, getting dirty and frequently drunk without having to think about the consequences. The world was huge and there'd been so many places he'd tried to lose himself.

"But did you enjoy it?" AJ asked.

"Yes. I met people, made friends." He paused, remembering. "One good mate who's now head of security at GEM. I did some amazing stuff."

"Like?"

Lord, when she smiled like that the tight ache in his heart eased. "I hiked the Andes, backpacked the Greek Islands. Biked around France, joined a rebuilding project on some dilapidated castle in southern Italy…"

Her sigh was envious. "See, that's my only problem with Australia—we're too far from the rest of the world."

He watched her methodically butter her roll then take a bite, releasing a small murmur of delight as her teeth tore into the bread. "Still love bread, huh?"

She nodded with a sheepish grin, demurely placing the rest of the roll on her side plate. "I'm surprised you remember. Most men I know have this innate ability to delete great chunks of information from their brains." She grinned, taking the edge off.

"Not me." He leaned in, extending one arm so his hand rested a bare millimeter from hers.

AJ tried—but failed—to ignore that hand so dangerously close to hers. "That's right. You're the only guy I know with total recall."

"Now *that* was a great movie. The original, not the remake."

She quirked her eyebrows. "I didn't know you were an Arnold fan."

"Oh, there's a lot about me you don't know."

"Like…?" It was out before she could stop it, before she could remind herself of her three rules.

Never count on anyone. Never get close enough to care. Never, ever get comfortable.

But she did care. She was only human.

He reached out, tracing one finger over her knuckles. "I sang at the Opera House once."

"Get out! You did not."

"Did so. It was a statewide school thing, with the best from each primary school choir performing for two nights."

"So you can sing."

He shrugged. "Not spectacularly, but yeah."

"Are you trying to impress me?" She smiled as the waitress arrived with their meals.

"Is it working?"

"Maybe."

He threw back his head and laughed, and the rich deep sound warmed her from the inside out. Lord, she'd missed that laugh. Missed the way his eyes creased at the corners, the way that sensuous mouth curved into something sinful.

She settled into eating her meal. The chicken was delicious, cooked in a creamy sauce with just a hint of rosemary and oregano. She took another mouthful and murmured under her breath.

"Good?" Matt asked.

She nodded. "You should try this." She'd already cut off a piece, offering her fork, when the memory hit. Another time, another place. Sharing one of many meals, getting through only a few bites before they'd given in to another craving. The food had been stone cold by the time they'd returned, flushed and physically sated.

He leaned in to take her offering. With a grin he chewed, eyes never leaving hers. "Delicious. Do you want to try mine?"

Yes. "Okay."

She was fully aware of his scrutiny as she parted her lips, slipped the steak in, then let the fork slowly ease from her mouth. The peppery sauce hinted at a few familiar herbs— pesto, basil, a little garlic. She nodded, swallowing. "Wow."

"Yeah."

The seconds lengthened, intimacy warming the moment. Shadows and light flickered over them and suddenly his eyes turned way too serious.

AJ broke his gaze and focused on her plate instead.

They finished their meals and the waitress arrived to take their plates. "Would you like to see the dessert menu?" she asked, stacking everything expertly on one hand.

Matt raised an eyebrow at AJ in silent question. She shook her head. The meal had dragged on long enough and her nerves were at breaking point.

"Coffee?"

She shook her head again, but Matt said, "An espresso would be good."

She glared at him as the waitress left but he just smiled. "Always in a rush, Angel. I remember that about you."

She leaned back in her chair and huffed out a breath. "You're doing this on purpose."

"Doing what?"

"Making me…" *Impatient. Aroused. Frustrated.* She clenched her teeth. "You know, you can be irritating sometimes, Matthew Cooper."

He leaned in. "*I* can be irritating? Let's see. I remember one particular night in my pool—"

"Stop."

"—when you performed a particularly frustrating strip-tease for me and—"

"Stop!" she hissed through her teeth. "Are you trying to embarrass me?"

"Ah, Angel. The fine art of teasing was never your strong point. At least," he added, his eyes glinting, "not verbally, anyway."

What could she say to that?

"I'm going to the bathroom." She grabbed her clutch and rose.

Teasing? I'll give him teasing. She deliberately put a sway in her hips, knowing Matt was watching every step she took. *Serves him right.*

She pushed open the door to the ladies' room with an exasperated huff. Was he punishing her—was that it? But why? Because she'd asked him to father her child? Because he was attracted to her and…what, he was angry about that?

Or was it something deeper? Something older…maybe ten years old?

AJ strode over to the long vanity and paused in front of the mirror. With one expert finger she smoothed her eyeliner, then dug around in her bag for her lipstick. *He'd* broken up with *her. He'd* moved on, gotten married.

Her reflection blinked back at her. If he could compartmentalize this, so could she.

Her heart contracted as she swept the Revlon lipstick across her mouth, then pressed her lips together. He'd not only gone through a demanding childhood, but he'd also had to deal with the death of his brother, turning that loss into the motivation for creating GEM, a major global rescue company. Drive and determination were two qualities that defined Matthew Cooper, no matter what he did in life. He wanted something, so he pursued it; his medical degree and GEM were proof of that.

Well, she was determined, too.

AJ capped the lipstick, smoothed her hair down, then scrunched the ends to boost the curl. "Time to move this thing along," she murmured, taking one last look at her vampy reflection before turning to the door.

She strode back across the crowded dining floor, ignoring the handful of men watching her progress. Only one guy was in her sights right now, and he was downing his coffee with the smooth efficiency of someone impatient to be somewhere else.

Alrighty, then.

When she stopped at their table, Matt glanced up.

"Are you ready to go?" she said. He took her in for only a second, maybe more, but it was enough to send a shiver over her skin.

"Yes." He abruptly stood, and she had to take a quick step back as he invaded her personal space. Then he reached for her hand, linking his fingers through hers, and her insides sent up a little cheer.

This was it. The moment she'd been waiting for all night. She was ready.

Nine

They barely made it to the car before he pushed her against the passenger door and kissed her.

The cool metal seared through her dress, a stark contrast to the warm hardness of eager male. He was in her senses, her every breath, her very blood. His kiss was so good, so hot. She had missed this, missed the familiarity of his touch, the way he boldly took control. She'd spent too many years controlling herself and having the chance to release that burden—even for a brief time—was such a welcome relief. And yes, he knew exactly what he was doing, from his hands cupping her bottom, to his mouth sliding across hers, to his questing tongue parting her lips and diving deep inside.

She moaned. Yes. *Yes.* So very good. So good she could hardly take the time to breathe for fear she'd miss something.

"Let's do this in the car," she whispered against his mouth.

He groaned. "Angel. We can't—"

"Of course we can," she said. Her hands went to his belt then crept lower, and she gasped when she encountered the hard bulge.

With an oath he wrenched his mouth from hers. "Not here."

"Why not?"

He sighed, gently placing his forehead on hers. "Because it's a public place and I don't want to get arrested."

Oh, yeah. She grinned. "Then let's go."

"Hello, Matt. Are you coming or going?"

AJ couldn't miss the way Matt's entire body suddenly tensed.

Then he inhaled, deliberately relaxed and turned. "Hi, Katrina. We're just leaving, actually."

Katrina. His ex-wife. AJ glanced past Matt, taking in the Amazonian ice blonde with amazing cheekbones. She was all legs, flat stomach and slim boyish hips, dressed in an oyster-colored knit dress and matching shoes, setting off her tan and thin arms to graceful perfection. Her bright green eyes returned AJ's stare.

She wondered what the other woman could see, whether she felt as gauche as AJ suddenly did.

Highly doubtful. She didn't appear to have a single unsure bone in her body as she stood there on the sidewalk.

"Who's your friend?" Katrina said now, offering a long-fingered hand. Soft skin, firm handshake, AJ noticed.

"AJ Reynolds, this is Katrina Mills."

"Nice to meet you," AJ lied smoothly, suddenly feeling way too loud and dramatic next to this elegant vision.

"Same here. Well." Her smile returned to Matt. "I have a date. Have a nice night."

"You, too." He nodded, watching her go with his hands deep in his pockets.

Finally, he turned back to AJ. "Sorry about that. I honestly didn't know she'd be here."

AJ shrugged, going for nonchalance. "It doesn't bother me. You said you were over, right? So you've got nothing to apologize for." She glanced back at Katrina as the woman disappeared into the restaurant. "She's gorgeous. I can see why you married her."

"Hmm."

What kind of answer was that? Stung, AJ slid into the passenger seat without a word, the mood well and truly broken.

They drove back to Matt's apartment, faint music from the radio filling the silence.

This was awkward. Way more than awkward—excruciating.

Was he thinking about Katrina? Was that why he'd suddenly gone from white-hot to cold? Worse, was he comparing them? And if so, did she come out the winner or the loser?

Matt jabbed a button on the radio and the music changed to some crazy club tune, heavy on the bass and light on originality. AJ stared out the window, her thoughts becoming grimmer.

When they finally drove into the parking garage, AJ turned to him. "What's wrong?"

He turned off the engine. "Nothing. Why?"

"Do you usually drive around in ominous, brooding silence? I'm a pretty good judge of mood, and you, Matthew Cooper, are in a pissy one. Is it your ex-wife?"

He swung open the door and threw a look over his shoulder just before he got out. *Bingo.* She followed suit, slamming the door and rounding the front of the car. "So it wasn't an amicable split?"

He clicked on the car alarm before turning to the elevators. AJ hurried to match his stride. "Oh, it was perfectly amicable." He sighed, punching the button. "Katrina is all about appearance, and our divorce was nothing if not polite and quick."

"So why—?"

"I have to deal with her on a monthly basis, which is once a month more than I'd like. She's Saint Cat's admin director," he added as the elevator doors opened and he walked in. "And my company depends on a mutual arrangement with their doctors and staff."

"I see." She followed him in and the doors slid closed.

"She's damn good at her job." He waved his key at the sensor and the elevator began to move. "My parents were thrilled when we got married. But she and I…"

"Weren't a good match."

"Not really, no."

She couldn't imagine Matt with someone like Katrina. He was too…passionate. Intense. Sensual. And Katrina looked like she could freeze an ice cube off her perfectly sculpted cheekbones.

So what had happened? Curiosity burned yet she let it simmer instead of putting it all out there. She didn't want to know. Talking meant sharing, sharing meant intimacy and intimacy meant...

No. Think about your goal. That's what you're here for.

Never count on anyone. Never get close enough to care. Never, ever get comfortable.

She shifted from foot to foot. Living by those three rules had protected her from the worst of everything—heartbreak, disappointment, setback. Yet after she'd reconnected with Emily and had started to put down tentative roots, those rules had begun to fray around the edges. Her sister had gradually earned her trust until she'd become the one person she loved more than anything in the world. Plus, she'd been sharing a three-bedroom house in Mermaid Beach with a corporate lawyer and her personal trainer cousin for two years, which, she had to admit, was pretty comfortable.

But those were anomalies.

The elevator doors slid open, and she followed Matt into his apartment.

She'd dated a psychologist for a while and apart from the annoying way he'd never bite back when they argued, he'd taught her a lot about the intricacies of human behavior and what drove people to do what they did. Yet knowing that, people still surprised her. Like now. Matt had been so into her at the restaurant, but now... He walked in, loosened his tie and headed straight for the kitchen without a backward glance.

Invisible much?

She sighed, suddenly at a loss. *And I even waxed...*

"Do you want a drink?" he called while she stood in the middle of the living room, contemplating her next move.

"Tea would be good." She glanced at the pristine chocolate-brown corner lounge and the smoked-glass coffee table. She'd been in his apartment less than a day and had already made her chaotic presence known with a water ring and a handful of smudges on the glass top.

"Do you have a cleaning service?" she called.

"No, why? Do I need one?"

She cast her eye around with a frown. "Not at all," she muttered. "You just—"

He emerged from the kitchen, tie askew and top button undone, revealing the inviting vee of his neck. She glanced away.

"What?"

Filter, AJ, filter. She sighed. "You need a little color to brighten up your walls is all."

He glanced around. "You don't like my place?"

"Well, it's nice. Elegant," she added. "I mean, I'm no Picasso, but I have a painting that would—" She suddenly snapped her mouth shut.

"What?"

She shook her head. "I can't believe we're discussing your decor right now."

His brow went up. "What would you rather be discussing?"

Her breath quickened and her eyes zeroed in on his neck again, then went back up to meet his eyes. "Nothing. I'd rather be *doing*."

Man, he'd forgotten how direct this woman could be! After years of office politics, international red tape, playing nice and pretending with the best of them, Matt had missed that directness. She told it like it was, one of the things that had drawn him to her.

"C'mere."

She was in his arms quicker than he could blink, lips tilting up, eager for his. With a groan, he obliged, slowly covering her mouth.

Yes. She welcomed him inside, teasing his tongue as she wrapped her arms around his neck, pulling him closer. The warm press of her breasts against his chest, her lean body and gently curving hips as they bumped urgently into his groin sent his pulse racing.

She murmured something low and encouraging, firing a spark deep inside his belly. Her thighs pressed into his, her arms tight around his neck as she angled her mouth so he could take her deeper.

And just like that, he was hard and ready to go.

"Matt," she gasped, pulling back to stare at him through passion-heavy lids. "Take me to bed."

Then she took his hand and placed it on her breast. The guttural growl came from deep in his throat, wrenching out one word. "Angel…"

He could barely think when her pebble-hard nipple pressed eagerly into his palm. Damn it, he wanted to take his time, seduce her the right way so she'd begin to trust him. A quickie in the middle of his lounge room was not a good place to start, even if it would satisfy his lust.

But it was hard to stop when she was rubbing up against him, the firm globe of her breast in his hand, her nipple erect and ready. His fingers convulsed and he let out a groan, curling them for one agonizing second around that wonderfully soft mound, then slowly dragging his palm across the engorged nipple. She whimpered, sighed and stretched her head back, exposing her long neck.

Furious need thundered through every vein, and he took a deep breath to steady his racing thoughts. Then another.

Plans had a way of derailing, and if he didn't put a stop to this he'd lose the ground he'd already gained. Even as his body screamed in protest, he released her and took a step back. Her eyes sprang open and the dark desire in those depths coupled with a soft moue of disappointment speared him right in the groin.

You can do this. "AJ, we need to—"

A sharp, familiar tune suddenly echoed in the heated silence.

AJ groaned. Her phone.

He frowned. "Is that…?"

"'Young Turks' by Rod Stewart. My sister's choice."

"Then you'd better get it," he said, taking another step back.

Are you insane? AJ gave him an incredulous look. "It can wait."

"Could be important." His expression was shuttered and the distance he'd created spoke volumes. She blinked, watching Matt stride back into the kitchen, undoing his tie as he went, and her confusion was magnified a thousandfold. Still, Rod continued to sing, and with a sigh she reached into her clutch.

"Do you know what time it is?"

"What, did I interrupt you getting ready to go out, Miss Party Queen?" Emily said.

"No." She turned toward the windows with a scowl. "And shouldn't you be doing something more interesting on your Paris honeymoon than calling me?"

"Zac and I had a bet. I thought my carrier had canceled my international roaming and he disagreed."

"You know you can check that in your settings, right?"

"And deny myself the pleasure of hearing your voice?"

AJ felt a reluctant smile form. "Well, tell Zac congrats, he won. Won what, I don't think I want to know."

"You hear that, darling?"

"Smart girl," she heard Zac murmur, then came a pause, followed by a giggle. AJ's heart twisted briefly before she brushed it off.

"If you've quite finished flirting with your husband, Mrs. Preston—"

"Hang on. You left a message about the apartment. How long do you need it for?"

"Not sure. A few months?" She toed off her heels and let her feet sink into the plush carpet with a sigh.

"What?" She heard her sister shift then mumble something to Zac. "What's keeping you in Sydney that long?"

AJ paused, then finally said with a wince, "A…man?"

"You don't sound too sure."

"I am. I think." She couldn't help it—she flicked a glance toward the kitchen. The man in question was exiting with two steaming cups, tie dangling loose and hair still sexily rumpled. She glanced away and shoved a stray lock of her own hair behind her ear.

"What about your stall?" Emily said.

"I can set one up at The Rocks."

"Hmm."

"*Hmm*—what?"

"Oh, nothing. But Zac's planning on having an open house so we'll need the apartment by October third."

AJ did a quick mental calculation. "Seven weeks away?"

"If you say so…" She ended on a gasp, then the phone clunked ominously in AJ's ear.

"I'm hanging up now," AJ called. "Bye, Zac!"

"Bye, AJ," came her brother-in-law's deep voice on the other end before the line cut out.

"Having a good time, are they?" Matt asked, placing her cup on the coffee table.

AJ nodded. "They're in Paris. Who wouldn't have fun?"

"How did they meet?"

AJ eyed him, tapping the edge of her phone gently on her chin. "He was her boss."

"An office romance, hey?"

"Something like that." Emily deserved to be happy. And Zac was perfect for her, despite their rocky start. Clandestine affairs didn't always turn out well, but theirs… Well, you only had to see them together to know they were completely and totally in love. "Emily planned the perfect wedding and the perfect honeymoon." She gave a small smile. "She's such an organizer—unlike me. She likes things just right. She's a true believer in love and romance and all that 'hearts and flowers' stuff."

"And you're not?"

AJ shrugged. "Oh, I believe in attraction, in passion. Love, sure. But fidelity? Soul mates?" She shrugged.

He frowned. "That's a bit cynical. What about the millions

of couples who've been together and stayed faithful over the years?"

"I didn't say it doesn't work. Just not for me."

"Why not? What makes you so different from anyone else, AJ?"

She scowled. "Our past defines us," she said tightly. "It makes us into the people we are."

"So you're saying you have no free will? That you'll let an event or person tell you how to think and feel?"

"No!" She scowled. "But people are conditioned for self-preservation. We're either in pursuit of things that make us feel good or protecting ourselves from hurt. And growing up, it was always the latter. My mother—" She abruptly clamped her mouth shut. That subject was a major mood killer. "Look, are we going to talk about my past or have sex?"

He took her in through hooded eyes as he slowly placed his cup on the coffee table.

She swallowed, realizing she'd said entirely the wrong thing.

"I have some work to do. I'll probably be up awhile."

Yep. Wrong thing. Flustered, AJ couldn't hide her disappointment, yet he didn't say a word, just pulled his tie free. "I'm leaving for Italy on Sunday."

"Italy?" she said, trying to ignore the sudden feeling of loss. "Lucky you."

He shrugged, folding his tie slowly and precisely. "It's for work. I don't have time to sightsee."

"Right." Work. It would always come first. She'd known from the start she'd have to fit in around his work schedule. But was it foolish to be just a little disappointed?

"Good night, AJ." He picked up his coffee then turned and strode toward his office.

She glared at the door as he closed it behind him. If that wasn't a rejection, she didn't know what was.

It was obvious that he wanted her. So why weren't they naked on his couch right now?

"Work," she muttered in the cool, dark silence. "Or the ex." Really, what other explanation could there be?

She stared at the carpet, hands on her hips. She had no reason to be angry, not when she'd actively pursued this arrangement. Hell, she should be thankful he was so work-focused because didn't that just make everything easier?

She huffed out a sigh and stared at the closed door. "Cold shower, I guess," she muttered, then turned toward the bathroom.

AJ rolled over in bed and stared at the faint light coming under her door. Was Matt still working? She grabbed her phone and squinted at the time. 1:17. Surely the man had to sleep sometime.

As she lay there in the darkness, surrounded by unfamiliar scents and silence, her mind sluggishly kicked in. Pretty soon it was full of too many questions, too many thoughts.

Too many doubts.

With a grunt, she tossed off the bed covers then grabbed her robe. When she eased her door open, the subdued living-room lamp cast shadows across the room, but it was Matt's office she focused on. She padded across the carpet, then placed her hand on the closed door.

Inside, she could hear his clear deep voice followed by another male voice that was slightly muffled and tinny. Skype? She heard Matt say, "Thanks. See you Sunday." Then nothing.

The gentle clack of fingers on keyboard punctuated the silence. She grabbed the doorknob and slowly turned it.

Matt was at his desk, a laptop open in front of him, the rest of the surface strewn with papers, pens, a file or two. He'd rolled up his shirt sleeves, revealing lean tanned forearms sprinkled with dark hair.

"Did I wake you?" he said suddenly, his focus still on the computer.

"I'm a light sleeper."

He reached for a paper, scanning it with a frown. "You should go back to bed."

She shoved a hand through her hair. "So should you. It's late."

He paused, placed the paper into a folder, then slowly swiveled his chair to face her. "In Rome it's twenty past five in the afternoon."

Rome. "Nice to know."

"Don't worry, I'll be back for our appointment."

"That's not what I was thinking." When he raised an eyebrow, she continued, "It's Rome. Home of the Trevi Fountain, the Sistine Chapel, the Vatican. All that wonderful history and art…"

He studied her, looking all comfortable and relaxed in his office chair, a curious smile on his lips. "You've never been to Rome?"

"I've never been outside Australia. Too expensive."

His gaze held her firm, revealing nothing. "Come here."

She eyed him back. "Why?"

"Why not?"

She took one step forward, then another, until she was standing barely a foot away. He reached out, snagging her robe and dragging her to him until she was trapped between his thighs.

She reached out to steady herself and when her hands met his shoulders, she felt him tense. Like an old motor starting up, her pulse began to pound, but this time it was panic of a different kind.

She waited, heart in her throat as his eyes held hers for long, agonizing seconds. Then, without breaking contact, he slowly, almost reverently, untied her robe, gently peeling it back like he was unwrapping a wonderful new gift. When his knuckles briefly grazed the curve of her waist, her breath stuck and her eyes widened. Then he slid his hands over her hips and glanced down.

He snorted, mouth curving. "Nice jammies."

"I happen to like Hello Kitty," she said in mock offense. "And they're comfy."

"Yeah, they look it. Very…" His gaze returned to her low neckline, to her breasts barely contained by the soft tank top. "Well-worn." And then he shocked her by reaching out and gently brushing his thumb over her peaking nipple.

Her breath hissed in. Their eyes met.

"I thought you said we should wait until after our appointment," she managed to say.

His eyes darkened. "Do you want me to stop?"

The air suddenly became too warm, too thick.

She started to lean in the exact moment he pulled her down. They met halfway, an eager joining of lips and breath. When Matt kissed her, the outside world dissolved.

With a groan, she closed her eyes and put all she had into that kiss. She welcomed his tongue when it roughly invaded her mouth. She murmured her acquiescence when his hand cupped her breast then teased her aching nipple into eager hardness. And she offered no resistance when he fisted his other hand in her hair, pulling her down. His roughness excited her, making her groin ache. Already her breath was coming out heavy, and as she went to her knees on the carpet, she reached for his shirt, fumbling for the buttons.

After a second—a long-drawn out, painful second—she muffled a curse and instead, ripped his shirt open. The buttons went flying but she didn't care. She just needed to feel his skin, trail her hands along his smooth chest, then follow it with her mouth.

He sucked in a breath when her questing fingers found his nipple. "Matt…" she purred, her smile widening at his guttural response. "Take me to bed."

Matt groaned. When had she managed to turn the tables on him? He was supposed to be in control, making the decisions here. He had a plan, a damn good one. Yet one kiss from AJ's lush mouth and he was panting like a dog in heat, prepared to let everything fall to pieces.

"We need to—"

"What, Matt?" She tweaked his nipple and he gasped, lust exploding in his belly. "What do we need?"

"We should—" He squeezed his eyes shut as her other hand descended, cupping his hard manhood.

"We should…" Her mouth parted again and he leaned down to take it like a thirsty man. She was so very hot, scorching him with her hands and lips and sweet body. He cupped her breast again, marveling at the lush curves on such a lean frame before pulling aside her tank top and releasing the glorious fullness.

He ripped his mouth free from hers and fastened his lips on her nipple with a satisfied groan.

Her gasp echoed off the walls as he tongued the nub, gently using his teeth and lips until it hardened beneath his ministrations. "You taste so sweet, Angel. So very sweet," he muttered, dragging his mouth across the soft globe, then rubbing his stubbled chin over her nipple.

He was rewarded with another gasp, and with lust thundering through his veins, his groin painfully hard and every sense eager and ready to go, he finally gave in.

He hooked his thumbs in her pants and swiftly pulled them down.

After a brief caress and an appreciative murmur, he gently spread her knees, his hand diving between her legs.

Her gasp sent hot, urgent desire flooding his senses, and when he felt her wobble, he placed a steadying hand on her, while with the other he parted her folds and firmly eased one finger into her damp warmth.

She trembled so sweetly, it was hard to get control, but he did, and when he slid his finger deeper, making deep circular motions inside, her voice gurgled in her throat.

"You like that?" he murmured, tipping her forward so his lips met her neck. She nodded her agreement, squeezing him inside.

He paused. "More?"

"Yes." It was a plea and they both knew it, but they were past the point of caring right now. He slowly pulled out before easing back in with two fingers this time.

The tightness made her gasp, her eyes widening as she stared right into his. They were dark like an abyss, passion bleeding them black.

Then he started to move, to glide in and out, and the delicious friction overtook everything else.

He gave himself over to pure sensation, to the smell of their passion, her gentle murmurs and heavy breath, to the way she rocked her hips as he gradually coaxed her higher and higher.

"Matt," she finally managed to gasp. "Please…faster!"

He did as she asked, diving deep, building the moment, teasing and arousing until inevitably, she was right there on the edge.

"Yes," he muttered, his mouth going to her breast again, teeth grazing her nipple.

And then he gently bit down and she exploded with a wrenching cry.

Matt clung to the last remnants of control as she enveloped him, the sensual beat pulsating, filling him to bursting. And then there it was, that gloriously sweet release when she came for him, when she was finally and irrevocably vulnerable beneath his hands. He'd done that and, damn, he felt like he could take on a whole army right now.

Except he was barely holding on and his erection was killing him.

With his hand still intimately holding her, he tried to undo his pants with one hand.

With a soft curse, he sighed. AJ shifted and suddenly her hands were at his belt, undoing it with deft fingers.

His grin matched hers until she hesitated, teeth nibbling her bottom lip as wide eyes met his.

"I can't do this with you…with me…" She shifted then and Matt got it. "Right."

Slowly, gently, he withdrew, and the sweet sound of her

breath hissing out and the sudden musky scent of sex permeating the air made his blood race. They exchanged a knowing look, a look of lovers who knew exactly what was to come.

He took in her passion-brightened eyes, the way her lips curved as she silently yanked down his pants and boxers. He kicked them off, peeled away the tattered remnants of his shirt then reached for her.

They both sighed, lips exploring each other for a brief moment until Matt guided her backward to the desk. Cradling her firm bottom in his hand, he lifted her up, sliding her across the top and scattering the papers and pens in the process. Then he eased her leg around his waist and sure enough, she knew exactly what he wanted her to do. She swiftly brought her other leg around, linking her ankles at the small of his back. Her heels dug into his butt and he repositioned himself, eyes locked on hers. Her breath puffed over his cheek as she leaned in, eager and ready, and his lips caressed the careening pulse in her neck, breathing in the glorious scent of her damp skin.

And then he plunged in and it felt like the whole world skidded to a standstill.

Thrum-thrum-thrum-thrum. The beat throbbed hard and loud in his ears as her wet tightness completely surrounded him, a sweetly painful yet glorious sensation that grew as he struggled for control.

He grabbed her thighs, fingers digging into her pliant flesh as he shuddered. In the back of his mind he registered the odd thought—*this desk is a perfect height*—until she reached up and kissed him.

He devoted a few moments to her mouth, then finally began to move, slowly at first, then with a steady rhythm she quickly picked up on. Her hips thrust to meet his. With a groan he tipped her, angling deeper.

Their shocked gasps came out as one.

"Yes," she murmured, her hot breath in his ear, lips nipping his jaw. "Yes."

Sweat slicked them as they slid together, skin on skin. Mus-

cles stretched and moved harmoniously until slowly a familiar tightness gripped his belly. Matt gritted his teeth, thighs
clenching, but still he kept going, blinded by AJ's passionate
words in his ear, her sweet breath on his neck and her soft,
pliable lips tilting up to receive his mouth. He kept going until
he began to feel the swell of orgasm build, rushing closer and
closer the more he sank into her hot, welcoming core.

"Angel…" he got out through gritted teeth. "I think—"

"Me, too," she panted, her eyes tight, face straining. "Please,
Matt, I need…"

He knew. He knew because he needed it, too. Time stood
still and all he could do was suck in a thick breath and focus
on her glorious expression as she finally, sweetly, came for
him a second time. With a triumphant cry Matt let himself
go, breath exploding like a drowning man coming up for air
as he spilled into her.

Everything vibrated, pulsated, and his skin felt like someone had ripped a layer off. He shifted, wincing as his calf
tightened painfully.

"You okay?" she murmured.

Oh, yeah. "Just a cramp." He stretched his leg, careful
not to disrupt her afterglow. He loved seeing her this way,
all pouty and languid, her eyes heavy and mouth curved in a
satisfied grin. Her belly slid across his, slick with sweat, and
he gently skimmed a hand over her damp flesh.

"You've filled out," he said, cupping her hip, taking pleasure in the warm skin.

"Are you telling me I've put on weight, Matthew Cooper?"

His gaze snapped up to her teasing expression and he returned her grin. "Yeah, but it looks good. A few more curves
here," he stroked her hip, then trailed back to her belly. "And
here. I like it."

She smiled, that luscious top lip teasing him. "You sure
know how to flatter a girl." Then she winced and shifted. "I
think my butt has fallen asleep."

He glanced over to the clock on his laptop. "Smart butt. It's past two. We should follow its example."

"Okay."

She moved again and Matt gritted his teeth, stilling her with a hand on her thigh. "Wait." As he slowly eased from her, she hissed through her teeth. "Did I hurt you?"

"No. It's just…" She ducked his gaze, demurely drawing her legs together. "A bit tender."

When he stepped back and reached for his clothes, AJ took the moment to regain her composure, sliding off the desk and grabbing her pants from the floor. She didn't embarrass easily, yet she felt that annoying flush creep up her neck.

No other guy could make her blush like Matt could.

With her robe resecured and her pajama pants dangling from her fingers, she paused, watching him pull on his tattered shirt. The lean muscles in his shoulders shifted as he pushed one arm through a sleeve, then the other. She drank in the view, dragging her eyes across his smooth chest and dark nipples, down to his trim waist and abdominal ridges, to finally stop at his belly button where that tantalizing line of hair disappeared into his pants.

Her mouth went dry and she quickly snapped her gaze away. "I'm going to take a shower."

He nodded then said softly, "Sleep well, AJ."

You're not coming with me? She bit down on that presumptuous question and instead managed a smile. "You, too."

She waited until he turned back to the desk and, feeling incredibly out of sorts and oddly dismissed, she withdrew.

The discontent grew as she padded down the hall, offsetting the still-present throb of their lovemaking.

There was no reason to be annoyed, none at all. She'd pursued this and now she was getting exactly what she wanted.

With that thought firm in her head, she pushed open the bathroom door and turned on the light. A shower would go a long way to making her feel normal, even though she suspected this was just the start of many abnormal days ahead.

Ten

Matt leaned back in his chair, rubbed his eyes and reached for his third cup of coffee in two hours. Bright afternoon sun speared through the dark clouds outside and he winced, grabbing the remote to angle down the blinds.

As the shadows lengthened in his office, he relaxed a little. He'd been at GEM since eight and, amazingly, he'd managed to block out last night and focus on his schedule, completing his work in record time.

Until he paused and let his thoughts wander.

Lips...hair...soft sighs...

He swallowed his now-cold coffee, determinedly ignoring the way his body stirred. AJ was like a drug, seeping into his blood and arousing him to that point of almost painful ecstasy. Sure, they'd always been pretty explosive together but not like this. This was something more, something hotter, more intense.

Something deeper.

He shoved his cup across the desk. And now that he had the taste for her again, he wanted nothing more than to explore every new curve, kiss every inch of skin and bring her to climax over and over.

His phone rang, breaking off those dangerous thoughts, and he reached for it with a relieved sigh.

"Hello, darling."

The familiar, oh-so-proper English voice washed over him.

"Hi, Mum." He stuck the phone in between his shoulder and ear and turned back to his computer. "What's up?"

"Katrina tells me you're off to Italy on Sunday."

"Did she?"

"Yes." Alicia Cooper ignored his irritation with practiced ease. "Could you call into Ferragamo and pick up a package for me?"

"More shoes?" He grinned, clicking on his computer screen then glancing over at his iPad as it synced.

"A woman can never have enough shoes," she replied loftily.

As his chuckle petered out, she said, "Katrina also tells me she saw you last night."

"Yeah."

"With a redhead."

His hand stilled on the mouse. "Yep," he said cautiously.

"What happened to that other one...the dark-haired publishing assistant...Lilia, wasn't it?"

"Nothing happened. We just went our separate ways."

Matt ignored his mother's silence, clicking the mouse and closing all the windows until only his schedule remained.

"What's her name?" Alicia finally said.

Ah. There it was. "AJ."

"Excuse me?"

"AJ. As in Angelina Jayne." His computer trilled, indicating his office manager was updating his schedule. "Look, Mum, I'm a bit pushed for time, so..."

"What does she do?"

He swallowed a sigh. God spare him from his mother's dogged determination to interfere in his life. Though Paige would tell him to give the woman a break. She'd lost one son already and Matt had chucked in a career she'd been heavily invested in since he was born. Maybe she just wanted to stay connected.

More like provide unwanted criticism.

"Well, Matthew?" she demanded now. "What does this woman do for a living?"

"She's an artist." The pause on the other end of the line told him so much, none of it good. "Look, Mum, I really have to go—"

"Fine," she replied coolly. "Have a safe trip." Yeah, she was pissed. Matt rubbed his forehead, smoothing out the frown lines.

"I will."

He hung up, his good mood now laced with irritation. He glanced through his emails, forwarding a few, saving some, deleting the rest, before finally pushing away from the desk with a sigh.

This would not do. With a firm set to his jaw, he reached for his phone and dialed.

"Dinner again?" AJ glanced at the clock on the wall above the dining table—twelve-fifteen—then at a muted Dr. Phil on the massive TV screen. She stretched her legs, placing them carefully on the coffee table and crossing them at the ankles, then leaned back into the couch. "You really don't have to, you know."

"Wear something for the water."

"What, a bikini?"

"No." She heard the amusement in his voice. "Something for an ocean breeze. I'll send a car for you at five."

She hung up and tossed her phone onto the couch cushion. Everything still pulsed from last night, a dull ache that had her staring at the ceiling with a goofy, self-satisfied grin.

He was wooing her. Why?

She rolled her neck, wincing as she felt the muscles pop and stretch. Because that's what he did. Along with his passionate intensity, this attentive treatment was part of his charm. For all his faults, she had to admit being the sole focus of Matt's attention when they were together was incredibly flattering, not to mention a massive ego boost.

Amazing he was still single, despite his breakneck work ethic.

She scrolled through her phone messages, answering Emily's, deleting a couple of spam. "Maybe he likes being single," she said aloud to the TV. Dr. Phil nodded sagely. "Maybe he's just not interested in marriage." No, that wasn't right—what about Katrina? "Maybe she ruined it all for him." Hmm. Yes, that sounded plausible. The woman looked as if she could give a guy ice burns in all sorts of awkward places.

"Or maybe…" She deleted a few more texts. "He's just shut it all down." Despite his declaration to the contrary, she'd seen his expression twist into a brief flash of grief and regret when he'd mentioned his brother. Her stomach clenched. Matthew Cooper with emotional baggage? That was a new one. He didn't seem the type to regret anything; he simply plowed through life, single-minded in his focus. He was a man of science, of medicine. Of cold hard facts. The kind of driven, ambitious guy the movies and TV portrayed with eerie accuracy. Yet he was also a guy with hidden depths, who believed in something as ephemeral as fate.

Huh. So they did have one thing in common, besides the sex thing—past hurts equaled an avoidance of attachment.

She didn't have a chance to think more on that because the very last text caught her attention.

Miss you. C U tonight?

Huh. Jesse had texted her at one-thirty last night. "Not a chance in hell," she murmured as she typed in her reply.

No. I don't date married guys.

She sent the text, then glanced back at the TV. Dr. Phil was talking to two teens and it was apparent they both had very different opinions about raising their child.

"Good ol' Dr. Phil," she said, swinging her legs to the carpet. "Where were you when my parental unit needed your sensible advice? Not that she would've taken it, mind you."

Her phone pinged.

2morrow then?

Ass. She scowled at the Android smiley, but the little green face merely grinned back at her.

Only if Nirvana get back together.

Resisting the urge to hurl her phone to the table—not good, considering it was made of glass—she instead gently placed it on the edge and stood. Jesse James Danson. Oh, how he'd loved playing up his outlaw persona, charming her with his wit and boyish smile one afternoon at her stall. And she'd been sucked in all right, recklessly promising to hand deliver her painting to what turned out to be his single guy apartment in Mermaid Beach. Her delivery had turned into coffee, then a week or two of phone tag, then suggestive texts, then finally, a month later, he'd coaxed her into bed.

She grabbed her phone and turned off the ringer for good measure. She wouldn't give that guy any more of her time. She had a date to get ready for.

The sleek white Commodore arrived dead on five, pulling up in front of the apartment as afternoon light bled into early evening. The uniformed driver got out and opened her door with a smile.

"How are you this evening, ma'am?"

"I'm good." She smiled and slid into the soft bucket seat, her stomach somewhere in the region of her throat. Nerves again? After last night? How could that be? Yet the butterflies, the absent tapping of her toe, the familiar song under her breath all pointed to one thing.

She buckled up as the driver got in and met her eyes in the rearview mirror. "To the Quay, is it?"

"I think so. Sorry, what's your name?"

"It's Kim, ma'am."

"Hi, Kim. I'm AJ. And please, no 'ma'am.'"

He smiled and nodded as he pulled away from the curb and switched on the stereo.

AJ watched the traffic as they made their way along Parramatta Road, the University of Sydney on her right, the former Grace Bros. building, which now housed the shiny Broadway shopping center, on the left. The last time she'd been in Sydney, she'd been working in a Pitt Street Mall coffee shop and house sharing with two surfers, a German backpacker and a sex phone worker. Yet as memorable as that time was, the music coming through the car speakers overshadowed it. The songs curled softly into her brain and took her further back, to the times when she'd been crazy, full of youthful recklessness and eager for seduction by a wicked smile and a pair of serious brown eyes.

When the third song came on she sucked in a breath and leaned forward. "Is this your CD?"

"No. Mister Cooper supplied it."

"Oh."

"You want me to turn it off?"

"No, it's fine." She tried to focus on the peak-hour traffic outside but it was no good. "I don't believe it," she muttered as "Sway" by Bic Runga finished and Collective Soul's "Run" began. It was the same playlist her boss at Arabelle's had piped through their system that summer ten years ago, playing it over and over until her coworker Maz had laughingly threatened to strike unless he played something— anything!—else. AJ ticked off the songs, drowning in the past as the car cruised down George Street: "How Will I Know" by Jessica Sanchez, "With or Without You" by U2, "Put Your Arms Around Me" by Texas and, yes, even Cliff Richard's "Miss You Nights."

Her sudden grin was reflected back at her in the car window. Her boss had been a huge Cliff Richard fan. And Matt had remembered.

He couldn't have known that that CD had become her soundtrack of misery, every single song either speaking of lost love, unfulfilled desires or new passion—"Heart & Shoulder" by Heather Nova, "Here We Are" by Gloria Estefan, "Always the Last To Know" by Del Amitri.

She smoothed back her hair and put those thoughts from her mind. Instead, she tried to focus on how much she'd enjoyed working those twelve months at Arabelle's, the casual camaraderie the staff had shared, the fun they'd had spending all their days off at the beach, then partying all night.

Melancholy rose. Hearing this music again made her miss them, a bittersweet emotion considering they'd all moved on with their lives and started their own families.

"In the Air Tonight" by Phil Collins came on and her smile returned.

God, she loved this song. The sexy, mournful guitar, the smooth, haunting lyrics. Then that heavy drum solo that seemed to come from nowhere. It was a hot, provocative song, designed for lovemaking.

Perfect for tonight.

She squeezed her thighs together and breathed deep, the music curling seductively in her belly until the car finally pulled to a stop.

When Matthew swung the door swung open, she couldn't stop her heart from tripping over itself. Just like last night, he offered his hand and she took it, letting him help her from the car with a smile.

He swept his gaze over her, taking in her strappy silver heels, long wraparound red dress with the plunging neckline and soft black cardigan she'd topped it with. "You look great." But when his eyes went to her hair, he frowned.

Her hand went to her careful coiffure. "What?"

"What's with your hair?"

"What do you mean?"

He nodded. "Why do you tie it back like that? Doesn't it give you a headache?"

"No." She smoothed it back, tucking a nonexistent strand behind her ear. "It's more efficient this way. Less annoying."

"You should leave it loose." And before she could reply, he had a hand in her hair and was digging out the hairclips she'd painstakingly positioned.

She twisted away. "Matt! No!" She patted the back, fiddling with the now-messy strands. "Damn it." She scowled at him. "You've ruined it."

"Then take it down."

A soft growl of frustration rattled in her throat. "Fine." She plucked out the pins, then undid the elastic. Her hair came tumbling down, the soft, freshly washed waves falling over her shoulders, making her shiver. With a scowl, she unclasped her clutch and dropped the pins inside. "Happy now?"

"Yes." When he gently rearranged the strands, fingers brushing her cheek, her irritation faltered, then fizzled out. He linked his fingers through hers and led her across the sidewalk.

They were at the Man O' War steps, a long jetty just around the corner from the Opera House. The sun had set behind them, leaving the Botanical Gardens in shadow. She nodded to a sleek cruiser tied to a berth as they walked down the wooden jetty. "Did you hire a boat?"

"No. It's mine."

"You own a *boat?*"

"Sure. It's normally moored at my house but I got my captain to bring it on down."

"Your captain." Boy, this night was getting more surreal by the moment. "Nice music in the car, by the way. You have a good memory."

"Comes from years of study. Good evening, Rex." He nodded to the captain, impressive in his white uniform and brimmed cap. "This is Miss Reynolds."

"Mr. Cooper. Miss Reynolds." Rex inclined his head, smiling. "Are you ready to cast off, sir?"

"We are."

AJ made her way tentatively across the drawbridge, Matt's steadying hand at her back, before finally stepping onto the deck. It was like being on one of Sydney Ferries' JetCats, but where the JetCat was equipped for public service efficiency, carrying hundreds of commuters per trip, this vessel was decked out purely for luxury.

She slowly walked into the cabin, marveling at the opulence. The huge interior was obviously for serious entertainment, from the wraparound glass windows displaying Sydney Harbour in all its glory to the polished wooden floors. A couple of inviting couches huddled around a huge plasma screen to her left, and to her right was an eating area with dining table and bar.

She turned back to Matt and nodded to the unset table. "I thought we were eating."

He smiled. "We are. Aft. And—" he glanced at his watch "—it should be ready now. Come."

He led her to the door at the rear of the cabin, one firm hand on the small of her back.

They emerged into the cold night as the rumbling engines overtook the gentle sound of waves slapping the hull. A glass partition extended along the aft rail, shielding them from the wind, and dead ahead a small table was decked out for two, complete with white plates, oversized wineglasses and candles flickering in huge glass lanterns. A long food warmer sat on one side, and on the other, a huge patio heater emanated a comforting glow.

Wow. The chauffeured car pickup, the music, the boat. And now this. He'd gone all out when she would have been satisfied with takeout on the sofa. Yet something inside her did a little dance at the effort he'd put in.

It was the little things, right?

The engines surged and the boat abruptly picked up pace,

cleaving through the harbor with a whoosh of water and spray. The deck listed beneath her feet and he took her arm, steadying her.

"You like?" His smile was perfectly enigmatic.

She nodded. "I do."

"Great. Let's eat."

If someone had asked her later what the meal was like, she'd be hard-pressed to remember it. Matt's presence overshadowed every bite. She barely felt the cold wind whipping around the boat as he served their meal, all the while keeping up a comfortable commentary about the history of Botany Bay and Fort Dennison, Sydney's first convict island.

When she finally emerged from her little bubble to glance down at her plate, everything had miraculously gone.

"Dessert?" He smiled, holding his wineglass gently by the stem.

"What do you have?"

His smile deepened. "Crème brûlée, strawberries and a decadent mocha mousse."

"The way to a girl's heart." AJ sighed dramatically. "But you know," she went on, tapping a finger on her chin, "I don't remember you ever offering *three* choices before."

"I was a struggling student."

"Matthew Cooper, struggling? Rubbish." Her grin took the sting out of her words and he answered it with one of his own. They sat like that for ages until her phone rang.

She dug it from her bag, glanced down at the screen, scowled, then switched it to mute.

Matt watched her but said nothing.

"No one important," she supplied, dropping it back into her bag. "So. Italy, huh?"

He nodded. "My plane leaves at seven in the morning."

"Your plane? As in your own personal plane?" At his nod, her eyes rounded. "Wow. I am so in the wrong job."

He shrugged. "It's a necessity. That way GEM isn't bound

by commercial airline schedules. I can leave within half an hour if I need to."

"Must be nice to take off on a whim."

He lifted his eyebrows. "Says the Queen of Impulsiveness."

"Yeah…" She sighed. "But not so much anymore. Tell me, Matt." She leaned in, her elbows on the table. "After all the places you've been, having your own private boat and plane… is there something you haven't yet achieved? Some particular goal that's always eluded you?"

"Of course."

"Name one."

He paused, his expression giving nothing away. "I've never backed a winner in the Melbourne Cup."

She snorted. "Winning a horse race is not a dream."

"Speak for yourself!" He looked affronted. "It's not just a horse race—it's *the* horse race."

AJ shrugged. "See, I never really got the whole racing thing. Just seems like you're throwing away good money."

"So you don't drink or gamble," he murmured, eyeing her over the rim of his glass. "I'm learning all sorts of things about you."

Her eyebrows went up. "What's there to learn? What you see is what you get, right here."

"Angel, you are one of the most secretive women I know."

"Oh, know a lot of women, do you?"

He made a moue of indifference. "Right now…? I can't remember a single one."

She felt her face flush again, and when he smoothly rose and offered his hand she didn't hesitate. As she stood, her thigh inadvertently brushed across his groin and he sucked in a breath.

"Sorry," she mumbled.

He shook his head. "Don't be."

Damn it. Why him? Why this instant and intense lust?

She had absolutely no clue.

Then he kissed her and she stopped thinking.

They stood there, leisurely exploring each other's mouths, tongue and skin, while the slow burn of desire steadily curled higher and the hint of cold night teased everywhere their bodies didn't touch.

"Matt…" she got out, her breath racing across his mouth. "I need to—"

"I know."

"—use the bathroom."

His crestfallen look was so comical she had to bite back a grin. But when he nodded and stepped back, the keen sense of loss she felt chased away any amusement.

"Inside, to the left."

She nodded. "I won't be long."

Come on. Get it together. Palms flat on the polished vanity, AJ stared at her reflection in the huge bathroom mirror. This gut-sucking passion, this breathless rush of being swept along by something bigger, was all familiar territory. He affected her with every single kiss, every single touch. He had magic hands—magic Matthew hands.

Surgeon's hands, so familiar with the human body, so familiar with healing, with giving life.

So familiar with her.

She straightened the towel on the rack. This was a good thing. It meant she could relax and enjoy herself, which was highly conducive to baby making. Stressing about it would be counterproductive.

Okay, so go out there and have a good time.

With a nod at her reflection, she smoothed the ends of her hair, tweaked the edges of her bra to plump up her breasts, then rubbed her lips together, the smooth glide of lipstick a time-honored confidence booster.

She left the bathroom, her heels ringing boldly on the polished wood. But when she walked outside, her confidence dissolved under the weight of Matt's loaded gaze.

"Your phone rang again," Matthew said as she walked over to the table. "Someone called Jesse?"

"The married ex," she supplied when she noticed his too-casual, I'm-not-going-to-ask look. "He's—" Her phone vibrated and AJ glanced down. "Speak of the devil." She grabbed it and pivoted, stalking to the railing for privacy. Unshielded by the partition, the cold night air blasted over her skin, whipping her hair. She flicked on the phone, then shoved a hand through the whirling mass, shoving it from her eyes. "What do you want?"

"Jay-jay! How are you doing, sexy legs?"

"Stop calling me that—it makes you sound like an idiot." His deliberate twist on her initials and that little pet name had been mildly cute when they were dating. Now it just made her want to smack him.

"So, I thought we could grab a drink tonight."

"Look, I told you we're over. Stop calling me," she hissed, shooting a glance back at Matt, who was leaning over the opposite railing, his attention seemingly absorbed by the dark water below. "Go back to your wife."

"Aww, babe, if we really were over, why're you still taking my calls?"

"Because you keep calling me, dumbass!"

His laugh rumbled down the line. "I miss that mouth! Especially when you did—"

She hung up. With a frustrated growl she stalked back to the table, then slowly, deliberately put her phone down when all she wanted to do was hurl it into the ocean.

She put a cold hand to her cheek and sighed. Her face was burning.

"Why do you still have your ex on your phone?"

Matt had turned back to her and she eyed him, cupping her other cheek. "So I know when to ignore his calls."

"He calls often?"

She shrugged. "Once or twice a month."

"Why don't you tell him to piss off?"

She gave him a look. "I have. He keeps calling."

"So get him blocked. There are laws against stalking, AJ."

"Yeah, I know." She sighed. "But then I'd have to visit the police, file an official report—" That was the biggie. Her parents had screwed with her psyche so well, drumming in that irrational fear of the cops so deep it had taken her years—and a good therapist—to overcome their conditioning.

Plus, there was the small matter of her criminal record....

Her phone rang again but this time, Matt beat her to it. "Jesse? Yeah, this is AJ's phone. Listen, you need to stop calling her," he said in that cool, clipped tone. He ignored her silently mouthed protest and turned his back on her. "She's not interested in jerks who cheat on their wives. So get over it and move on." He paused. "Me? Dr. Matthew Cooper, former head of neurosurgery at Saint Catherine's."

"Oooo, a *doctor!* And *British,* too!"

Oh, Lord, she could hear Jesse's mocking comeback from here! And judging by the way Matthew's expression turned carefully blank, he was not impressed, either. His eyes locked on hers as Jesse let fly with something she couldn't quite make out.

Finally, Matt said softly, "Yeah, okay. I'd be careful who you're threatening, if I were you." Another pause, then a slow smile bloomed, his direct gaze still on her. "Because my best mate is ex-CIA and he really, really loves his guns. So be a good boy and lose AJ's number."

With that, he hung up and handed her phone back.

Honestly, she should be furious he'd butted in, but all that came to mind was… "Do you really know someone in the CIA?"

"He's my head of security."

"Right. But he wouldn't really shoot him."

"Who knows? Decker's been in some tight situations where force was the only option. We both have."

"So your job is dangerous then?"

"It can be." He reached for her hand and drew her close. "Why? Are you worried?"

"No."

She glanced away but Matt, damn him, had her measure. He pulled her flush against him, his heat searing into her, his laugh a soft breath against her cheek.

"You'd miss me, Angel. Admit it."

"Well, I wouldn't miss your huge ego, that's for sure."

"Ahh, but you'd miss this, I bet." Then his lips swooped down to meet hers and she just about melted on the spot.

They kissed until they were both breathless, until she felt her legs go wobbly and Matt gently drew her toward the cabin doors. Then they were inside and after a few more agonizing kisses, AJ felt a soft pressure on the back of her legs.

The sofa.

Matt nudged her and she sank into the cushions, taking him with her. He sprawled across her lap, his thighs hard against hers, his arms against the backrest on either side of her head.

"The windows—"

"Tinted," he got out, nipping her jaw.

"But the crew—"

"Topside. With instructions not to interrupt."

"But—"

"Angel, do you want to keep talking or would you rather I do this?" And with one smooth movement, he swept aside her dress and brought his mouth down to her breast.

Her back arched as he tongued her nipple to painful erectness through the black satin bra. Then he dragged the cup down, exposing her fully to his careful ministrations. His teeth latched on to that swollen nub and her breath hissed out in glorious ecstasy.

Oh, yes. She'd miss this. He was so very, very good at arousing her, whipping her into a bundle of aching, raw nerves until she was begging him to take her. Like now. She squirmed, eager for more of his lips, his tongue, his hands.

Pinned by his thighs, the bulge between them only frustrated her, fueling her desperation.

"Just so you know," she began, "this…ah…is going to be…" Another small groan escaped her as he dragged her dress off one shoulder and flicked his tongue along the exposed flesh. "It's just a simple matter of…"

"Want." There was no triumph, only complete conviction in his reply. Then he lifted his head, grasped her face firmly in his hands and silenced her with a kiss.

It was the best kiss she'd had in her life, and it just went on and on.

Finally, when they were both breathless, he released her mouth and returned to her breasts, gently sucking one nipple as he slowly massaged her other breast with his hand.

She groaned. "Matt…I need to move."

He shifted his weight, allowing her to wrap her legs around his waist.

"Would you miss this, Angel?" he murmured against her breast.

She muttered her ascent, too consumed with sensation to form a coherent word.

"And this?" He squeezed her other breast, kneading, caressing.

"Mmm." Her head lolled, eyes closing, and she heard his soft chuckle, full of male satisfaction.

"Or maybe this?" His hand went to her thigh, dragging her dress up. "You're so warm."

Their gazes locked. A wolfish smile gradually transformed his features, and AJ marveled at the sight. He was so beautiful. So totally and utterly seductive. So—

He pulled aside her knickers and dove into her folds, his thumb brushing over the hard nub.

Enough thinking. She let sensation take her. With every touch of his tongue on her nipple, every stroke of his fingers between her legs, her body jerked, pleasure sparking then fanning out, following the path of her blood as it chugged through her veins.

"Matt!" Ripples of desire sensitized her skin. "Please!"

"You seem to be doing a lot of begging lately, Angel." His voice practically purred as his fingers continued their excruciating work. "What would you say if I did…this?"

One finger slid into her slick heat and she gasped. *Oh, yes.* She waited…waited…

He'd stopped.

What the hell…? She groaned, wriggled around, trying to get him to move. Yet he remained still, his other hand flat on her belly, firmly holding her in place. Her breath raced, blood throbbing as she snapped her head up to meet his glittering gaze.

"Or maybe…" he said, his mouth kinking up into a wicked smile. "This?"

And in one smooth movement he slid down her body, removing her underwear as he went. Then he replaced his fingers with his lips and she nearly bucked off the sofa. White-hot sensation exploded as his tongue began lavishing attention on the most intimate part of her, licking, sucking, loving.

Desire throbbed through every single vein, every muscle in Matthew's body. AJ surrounded him—her skin, her scent, her soft moans of pleasure. It made him want to rip off his clothes and take her hard and fast on the floor. Yet instead of giving in to that desperate need, he took a jagged breath, gathered the threads of his shredded control and focused on loving her with his mouth.

He nibbled her inner thigh, dragging his chin across the sensitive skin. His fingers dug into her skin as he lifted her hips to him and feasted on her sweetness, running his tongue slowly up, then down, loving the way she tasted, loving that her scent and arousal were in his every breath. And when he felt her trembling slowly increase, felt her thighs tense around him, he knew she was heading to the edge.

He left her there, legs spread with her dress rucked around

her waist, one breast exposed, head flung back in a familiar arch of ecstasy while he quickly pulled off his clothes.

It took too long, way too long.

When he was finally naked, he positioned himself between her legs, his hands splayed on her rib cage, feeling her deep panting breath, the ripples of passion across her skin.

"Angel," he ground out. "Look at me."

She did, slowly, languorously, and the arousal in her eyes blew him away. With a groan, he plunged deep inside her.

He made love to her that way, his hands gripping her waist, their eyes locked, as he slid deeply in, then slowly out.

His pounding heartbeat echoed in his head, his chest. Damn, it felt so good! Better than anything he'd ever experienced in his life. He groaned again as she tipped her hips, and when she reached up and wrapped her arms around his neck, he let her pull him down. She kissed him, deeply, passionately, using her tongue to tease, taste, toy. His breath galloped, matching hers, the throb of their hearts pounding in unison as he plunged into her. And gradually, everything built, sweeping closer and closer until he couldn't stand the mix of agony and ecstasy any longer.

He thrust a hand between them, where their bodies were slick with passion and friction, his fingers seeking her tight bud. When he found it, she shuddered, eyes wide, as he flicked it over and over.

"Matt!" She gasped, her breath coming out in tight little puffs as her legs squeezed his waist. "I think…"

"C'mon, Angel," he crooned in her ear, his lips against her damp hair. "Come with me."

When she did, it was the most glorious thing he'd ever seen. It was so intense, so powerful, that his teeth clenched, jaw grinding as waves of pleasure rushed him, tossing him up then quickly dumping him down, down, so deeply down.

Everything screamed, every muscle, every vein, every inch of his skin. *Hot. Too hot. I can't…* Then sensation took over and with a wrenching groan he spilled into her hot warmth.

"Angel," he groaned, her slick heat surrounding him, accepting him, taking all of him.

Glorious.

Eventually, when he slowly began to return back to earth, his other senses kicked in. He took in her racing breath, her musky skin, the aftermath of her orgasm still pulsing around him. He'd done that, brought her to the peak of ecstasy, had made her beg for him, before taking them both over the edge. And man, he felt like leaping up and punching the air like some macho alpha, smug in the knowledge he'd thoroughly pleasured a woman.

Not just a woman. *This* woman. His arms tightened around her, skin still moist with sweat. Her chin was tilted up, her eyes shut, hands provocatively splayed across her neck, just above her breasts.

He dropped a gentle kiss on one peaking nipple and she started. He grinned as she glanced down to meet his eyes.

"You okay?"

Man, that smile undid him every time: languorous and thoroughly sated, full of warm pleasure. "Oh, yeah."

He bathed in the satisfied glow and let the silence surround them, a silence punctuated by the faint hum of the engines and the gentle rocking of the boat as it cleaved through the choppy Sydney waters.

"What time is it?" she finally asked, then suppressed a shiver.

He glanced over to the entertainment unit at the glowing DVD clock. "One. Why?"

"Shouldn't you be getting some rest before your early flight?"

"I can sleep on the plane." He looped his arms around her waist to gather her close but stilled when he felt her gentle tug of resistance.

Okay. That was odd.

Smothering a frown, he eased back, then slowly, regretfully, slid from her.

Whatever she was thinking, it wasn't good, given the prolonged silence while he gathered up his clothes.

When he'd dragged on his pants and turned back to her, she'd fixed her clothes and was now sitting demurely on the couch, knees pressed together, staring thoughtfully at her hands. Almost as if by meeting his scrutiny she'd inadvertently divulge something she'd rather keep private. And judging by her expression, she'd rather make a swim for the shore than tell him what she was thinking right now.

Steady on. This isn't some kind of race. And this was AJ—a woman who heated up his bed, gave herself so completely to their lovemaking, yet managed to keep a part of herself untouched.

The desire to break down her walls had never been as intense as it was right at this moment.

"You know," she finally said, meeting his eyes. "I never did get that dessert."

His sudden bark of laughter made her lips curve in response, and the tension leeched out.

"Then we shall have to fix that."

He offered his hand and she took it without hesitation.

Eleven

AJ awoke slowly in her darkened room, checked the time—nine—then rolled onto her back to stare at the ceiling. She'd left the curtains open last night and now the gathering storm clouds were obvious. A perfect start to a dingy day.

Matt had been gone for hours and he hadn't even said goodbye.

At six she'd heard him turn on the shower, then turn it off barely five minutes later. He'd moved around in the kitchen, then she'd finally heard the front door gently close at half past.

He was under no obligation to say anything, even if she was his houseguest. Even so, his absence of manners nettled her.

"Oh, for heaven's sake, stop with all this emotional stuff," she said sternly in the cool silence. "This is what we want, right? Matt to remain work-focused and you to concentrate on making a baby."

A baby. Her hand slipped down to the flat plains of her belly. It was way too soon, of course. She wasn't even ovulating yet. Still…she gently palmed her stomach, forbidden excitement rising as she glanced down. "Just don't take too long, okay?" she whispered. "Because I'm really not sure how much of Matt I can handle when he gets all focused and intense."

She lay there for a few more minutes, bathing in last night, flushing at certain memories and grinning at others. Finally she sighed, tossed off the covers and headed for the shower.

Today was the perfect day to move back into Zac's apartment. And no doubt Matt would be happy to reclaim his space, too.

* * *

Two hours later she shoved the key in the door to Zac's apartment and stumbled through. Everything about this twenty-fifth-floor penthouse suite drew her in, from the huge panoramic view of Potts Point, Centrepoint, the Harbour Bridge and Rushcutters Bay to the vibrant sunflower yellow interior walls, sleek blond furniture, colorful cushions and tangerine rug in the center of the polished wooden floor. But it was the massive living room that drew a smile every time.

Zac had framed and strategically hung her paintings along the huge feature wall there. She remembered every gentle, colorful mark of her watercolor pencils, the damp brush strokes that brought the scenes to life—Coogee Beach with its beach towels, umbrellas and crashing azure waves. A Sydney cityscape bathed in an orange and purple sunset. And Circular Quay, complete with busy ferries and peak-hour commuters against a Harbour Bridge backdrop.

"Hello, gorgeous things." She grinned as she dropped her bags inside the door and kicked it shut. "Miss me?" She cocked her head, her gaze going from one picture to another. "Of course you did. Well, the good news is, I feel like painting. The bad news? No paints." She dug around in her shoulder bag and plucked out her sketch pad, then a pencil. "Still, better than nothing, right?"

After fixing herself a cup of Earl Grey, she dragged the blanket off the couch arm, wrapped it around her shoulders, then padded to the patio doors. With a whoosh and blast of cold air, she walked out onto the balcony, settled in a comfy chair and began.

AJ formed a routine of sorts for the next few days —she rose at eight, swam a few laps in the heated rooftop pool and lifted weights for half an hour in the fourth-floor gym. Then she had breakfast, followed by sketching, and lunch from one of the many restaurants that occupied the ground floor. After lunch she went walking, undeterred by the weather's sudden return to midwinter temperatures. She made her way down William Street, poking around in the funky boutiques and secondhand stores, admiring the baubles and handmade clothing, then crossing over Crown Street and heading toward Hyde Park. Turning right on College Street, she headed east, toward the New South Wales Art Gallery.

She spent all afternoon soaking up the rest of the amazing art and doing a few sketches before heading back, only detouring for her usual Starbucks grande latte and a chicken sub.

On Tuesday night, Matt called.

"So what have you been doing the past few days?" Just hearing that low, cultured voice in her ear was enough to make her body quiver.

"Oh, you know, living the life of luxury. Sketching, walking. I missed the Van Gogh exhibit at the art gallery by a day."

"Bummer."

"Yeah. He's one of my favorites." She started to sharpen a pencil. "When are you back?"

"I fly in late Wednesday night."

"Okay." She added the finishing touches to her drawing—a view of the sunset-strewn Queensland hinterland from the seventy-eighth floor of the Q Tower. "Oh, by the way, I'm at Zac's apartment."

A small moment of silence passed, way too long to blame on the time delay.

"Why?" Matthew finally said.

She paused and stared out the window, watching a slow-moving ferry glide along Botany Bay. "Because that was my plan, remember? Besides," she added lightly, "I make a lousy houseguest, leaving my wet towels on the floor and hogging all the bathroom bench space."

Another too-long silence. "I wouldn't know. You never stay long enough for me to notice."

Her breath came out sharp. "Wow. That was a bit harsh."

She heard him sigh down the phone. "Sorry. Look, it's been a long trip and I just want to get home. I'll send a car to pick you up tomorrow and I'll meet you at Saint Cat's for our appointment."

"Matt—"

"I have to go. See you on Thursday." And he hung up.

She slowly clicked off her phone, head churning. What on earth was that about? Again he'd brought up their past, which meant it must be bothering him more than he cared to admit.

It's just not working for me, AJ.

Despite the passage of time, that statement still made her wince. He'd made the decision to break up and there was nothing more to be said. So of course, retreat had been her best course of action. She'd simply nodded, risen on unsteady feet and left.

And he'd let her go.

But she needed to stop analyzing this and focus on her appointment. Emily was the deep thinker of their little family; her endless pros and cons list was something AJ ribbed her about all the time.

Sadness bloomed for one second, making her sigh. God, she missed her sister, missed her overwhelming optimism, her unique outlook on life. Her logical advice.

What would she say about this arrangement?

AJ scowled. Eventually she'd have to tell Emily what was going on. That is, if Zac hadn't already.

At any rate, she had a two-week reprieve to practice before they returned. With that thought, she picked up her abandoned pencil, turned the page and began a new sketch.

True to Matt's word, a car arrived at eight-thirty the next morning and took her across the Harbour Bridge to Saint Catherine's Hospital, set in the exclusive north shore suburb of Kirribilli.

The hospital still looked shiny and new even though it was almost twenty years old. She'd read about the amazing leaps in medicine and research they'd made there throughout those years, along with all the other achievements: best heart surgery team in Australia, a crack cancer research facility. And of course, the addition of a new wing, opened by the Prime Minister herself—the Alicia Cooper Neurosurgical Unit.

Matt met her at the entrance with a smile, and before AJ could steel herself, her heart did a little skip. Then he removed his sunglasses. "Hi, Angel. How've you been?"

"Nervous." It was the truth. She'd been riddled with worry all the way across town, and a lot of it had to do with Matt. Despite all that inner talk, all that "this is just a deal, nothing personal" stuff, she was genuinely elated to see him again. Giddy almost.

"Don't be," he said, laying his hand gently on her elbow as they walked to the bank of elevators. "Dr. Adams is the best. Which reminds me, I have to tell you something before we go in."

"Yes?"

"It's going to come up in the consult. I had leukemia when I was seven but I've been in remission for close to thirty years. Don't worry," he added, misinterpreting her shocked expression. "This strain isn't hereditary."

"That's not what I was thinking." *Holy crap.* He had *cancer?* She paused, searching for something, anything, to say. "Are you okay?"

"Never better."

"Good." *He's okay. No reason to panic.* Then in the next moment she felt a small stab of hurt—why hadn't he told her this before? Still, her expression must have given her away because he glanced at her and frowned.

"Don't look at me that way."

"What way?"

"It's not a big deal. I don't need your pity."

"It's not pity."

He said nothing, just reached into his jacket, checked his phone and shoved it back.

It's okay, AJ. He says he's clear. She fiddled with her hair, tightening the knot at her nape. Leukemia was serious. Should she ask how—?

"AJ? Are you listening?"

Not when you drop that bomb in my lap, I'm not. But just as she was opening her mouth, he shut her down.

"Look, it's over, I'm healthy and let's just move on, shall we?"

He wanted to move on. It's what she did, right? It's what she was an expert at. With a sigh, she shifted gears, her mind reluctantly clunking into second as she focused on the long corridor, her loud footsteps as they made their way to the elevators dragging her away from the scary thought of Matthew's mortality. He'd put his hand on her back, and the contact was reassuring. Almost natural.

Of course, there was nothing natural about this arrangement, but she didn't want to dwell on that. All her nervous anticipation took a backseat when they were given forms and she had to switch her focus to the barrage of personal questions: about her parents, their parents, Emily, their health, her health, allergies, drug use. A vague feeling of disquiet rose until a door opened and Dr. Adams arrived to take them through to her office.

As the doctor talked, AJ felt herself warming up to the friendly, middle-aged woman sporting a shock of closely cropped white hair and a wonderfully calming disposition. She skimmed both their forms, then went through the list of tests AJ needed, including an ultrasound and laparoscopy. Then she did the same for Matt.

Dr. Adams had just booked AJ in for her tests when Matt's phone rang. He excused himself and went outside to take it, leaving AJ with the doctor. She didn't mind, not when she had so many questions. She was only halfway through when Matt walked back in.

"I'm sorry," he said, his brow dipping. "I have to leave."

"Everything okay?" AJ asked.

"Auckland was hit by another quake. I'm flying out in an

hour." He turned to Dr. Adams and they shook hands. "Email me the report, Sandi, and let me know when I need to schedule my tests." Then he turned to AJ, leaned down and, to her surprise, kissed her cheek. "I'll be back on Saturday."

She nodded, not trusting herself to speak. It was pointless to feel cheated but damn it, she couldn't stop herself from going there. Then Matt was gone and she was left with a vague feeling of loneliness congealing in her belly.

"Well." She turned to Dr. Adams with an overly cheerful smile. "Where were we?"

Twelve

When Matt returned on Saturday, AJ had given herself a serious talking-to, boxed up all those stupid fears and returned them to their dark corner. She'd spent Friday being poked, prodded and scanned, having blood drawn and being quizzed endlessly about her medical history. Then she'd spent the rest of the night researching the drugs Dr. Adams had mentioned, downloading a fertility schedule and checking her favorite boards and forums for updates. Her situation was not unique: lots of women were forgoing the "fairy-tale family" scenario to embark on single parenthood, and she'd connected with a few via a private chat room months ago. She'd read so many incredible stories and felt such wonderful support from these women that she was almost tempted to go into more detail about her own situation. But something always held her back, even when she'd met up with one of the mothers from the chat room for a long lunch in the Queen Victoria Building earlier that day.

As they'd said their goodbyes on the Town Hall steps at four, AJ's phone rang.

Matthew. Her heart did a weird little skip and suddenly, their evening on the boat came surging up again. It'd been foremost in her dreams the past few nights.

She stopped in her tracks, George Street commuters flowing around her. "Hello, Matt."

"Hi, Angel." His voice caressed her, made her all crumbly inside.

She squinted into the slowly spreading sunset and tried to rein everything in. Her first fertility injection had kicked in, creating havoc with her emotions.

"Hi," she repeated.

"Where are you?"

"Town Hall." She glanced around at the bustle and scurry of people. So serious, so focused on their phones, their destination, their purpose. "Where are you?"

"About twenty minutes away. Wait there—I'll pick you up. I want to show you something."

"Is it dinner again? Because I'm not dressed for it."

"Not dinner," he replied. "See you soon."

She hung up, anticipation quickening her pulse. He was back and she felt like doing a little jig right there in the middle of the street.

It's just the hormones. Her chat room friends had been brutally honest: increased desire was one topic that always cropped up. Her body ached for Matt like he'd been gone for months, not days, and she could acknowledge that fact and proceed accordingly, or make herself crazy worrying about the emotional implications.

Except the doctor had advised against sex, so that avenue of release was no longer a consideration.

She growled under her breath and glared at the passing people as irrational anger swelled inside.

Last week had been wonderful but also incredibly tense, leaving her with way too many raw emotions. Not a good thing. On the scale of importance, she ranked well below his career. She certainly didn't want to spend the rest of her life with him, not when she would never come first.

But what—?

No. She needed to focus on the plan, not poke holes in it. Provided they still *had* a plan. Given the doctor's recommendation, Matt could very well decide to change his mind.

She adjusted her scarf and shoved her hands deeper into the pockets. Well, she'd know soon enough.

* * *

Fifteen minutes later, she spotted Matt's car approaching. When the lights changed and the traffic stopped, she quickly threaded her way through the pedestrians and got in.

"Hi," he said with a grin.

"Hi, yourself." She slammed the door and buckled up, trying hard to ignore the giddy catch to her voice. "So, how was your trip? I was watching everything on the news."

"It went well. We recovered most of the missing and worked out a long-term rebuilding plan with the local services." His gaze returned to the road as the lights changed. "How did the meeting with Sandi finish up?"

"Did you get the report?"

"Not yet."

"Right." She tipped her head as he pulled to a stop at the lights at George and Bathurst. "So you don't know Dr. Adams said we should—mmmmph!"

He cut her off with a rough kiss.

It was unexpected but definitely not unwelcome. He just put a hand behind her neck and pulled her in, the move shockingly arrogant yet incredibly sexy.

She'd missed him. Despite the stern talking to she'd given herself, she'd actually missed him.

Or maybe she just missed this.

When he palmed her cheek with his other hand, her breath stuttered.

Yeah, that was it.

Finally—regretfully, it seemed to her—Matt pulled back, gave her a lingering look then returned his attention to the lights. They changed a second later and he turned into Bathurst Street.

"How are you feeling?"

"Hot."

His mouth curved, teasing out the dimple. "I meant that as an inquiry into your general well-being."

"Oh. Still hot." *And excited. Aroused. Wanting to—*

"Has Sandi started you on hormone injections?"

Someone blasted a car horn and Matt smoothly avoided a car braking in front of them. AJ nodded. "Yes."

"And I'm scheduled for some tests on Monday, correct?"

"That's right. And Matt…"

"Yeah?" They turned right on Elizabeth, heading west.

"She also said artificial insemination was our best option." The brakes tamped for one jerky second before they pulled into the Liverpool Street merge lane. AJ forged on. "Given my low chances of conception, apparently it's better to do this in a controlled environment. So there's nothing left to chance."

"Of course."

Another moment passed. "Which means after insemination, we can't have sex."

He pressed his lips together. "I know what it means."

They merged into the traffic and her heart began to pound. He wasn't happy and she couldn't blame him. But did that mean he'd go back on their deal?

She huffed out a breath and turned to stare directly ahead. "Matt, I have to ask…does this change things for you?"

"In what way?"

"Well, it's not exactly what you signed up for."

"You think I'd back out because we can't have sex?"

"I…don't know."

He sighed, his disappointment clear in that small exhale. "The answer is no." He shot her a look, then turned back to the traffic. "I gave my word, AJ. You can trust me."

"Okay." She nodded, taking a few slow breaths while she waited for her heart to calm down.

Silence spread until they stopped at another red light.

"Do you have a passport?" he asked suddenly.

She raised her brow. "No, why?"

"How do you feel about Portugal?"

"How do I…?" AJ frowned. "I don't know. They speak Portuguese? They're part of the European Union? Oh, and I've heard the Algarve Coast has a stunning coastline—"

"I'm due to fly out to Faro next Saturday." The lights changed to green, Matt eased into First and they turned left on College. "I'd like you to come with me."

What? "But I don't have a passport."

"I know some people. I can get one for you in a few days."

Of course he knew people. That shouldn't be a surprise. But what stunned her more was the fact that he was asking her to go with him.

"Isn't this a business trip?"

"Yes. But I'm the boss, so I can do whatever I want." His brief glance had her heart rate picking up most alarmingly. "You've never been overseas. So let me take you."

"But your work—"

"—will be finished in a day or two, max."

AJ shook her head, jamming a lid on her swelling excitement. "I don't want to interfere."

"You won't be." The traffic slowed and they crawled past Hyde Park. "The flight leaves at eight on Saturday morning. We refuel in Singapore, fly on to Rome, then land at Faro airport Sunday night. My meeting's Monday afternoon, so we can fly back on Friday. Is five days enough?"

Enough for what? "What are we going to do for five whole days?"

"Oh, I'm sure we'll think of something."

"Matt, I don't think we should—"

"This isn't about…that." She saw his jaw tighten almost imperceptibly as he kept his eyes on the road. "Look, if you don't want to go, just say so."

"I do!" she blurted, then more calmly added, "I do. But…"

"But what? You get to see another country, catch some sun, charge room service and relax by the pool. All good for your stress levels. Which, in turn, increases our chances of getting pregnant."

Our chances. Not *your.* AJ swallowed a small moan. Deliberate? Or a completely innocent slip?

Think about it. Five whole days in his company, sharing

meals, sightseeing and doing touristy things. Normal holiday couple things. Things she'd never pictured him doing, let alone with her. The Matthew Cooper she knew would never allow anything to interfere with his work schedule.

Maybe he's not the Matthew Cooper you remember.

She gazed contemplatively out the windshield. No, that wasn't right. Sure, he was no longer head of neurosurgery at Saint Catherine's, but a man like Matt didn't just turn off that blinding drive and determination to achieve. It made him who he was, and his company was tangible proof of that.

"Five days—" She suddenly broke off to stare out the window. "Wait, are we going to the art gallery?"

"Just wait and see."

"Matt. It's kind of obvious. Unless…" They drove down Art Gallery Road, the expansive grassy Domain parkland on their left, the familiar columned majesty of the art gallery entrance on the right. "There's nothing at the end of this road except Mrs. Macquarie's Chair." When she'd been a Sydney sider, she'd frequently enjoyed the stunning harbor views from that historic chair, which had been specifically carved from a rock ledge for Governor Macquarie's wife.

He found a vacant spot and smoothly pulled the car in. "You were right the first time."

"But it's closing in—" She glanced at the clock on the dash. "Ten minutes."

"Not for us it isn't."

He switched off the engine and turned to face her, sliding up his sunglasses. His expression was casually neutral, but she sensed something else in those dark, hooded eyes. A question? No, he was *waiting* for her. She could feel the expectancy heat the air, spreading gently as his gaze held hers.

She hadn't given him an answer to the Portugal thing.

A small bubble of excitement rose inside her. *An actual trip overseas!* She'd finally get to see another country, another culture, experience the sights, the smells, the tastes. She'd have a chance to observe color and movement, to stretch her drawing skills.

How could she pass this up?

She nodded, biting down on her lip to stop a goofy grin from forming. "Okay. I'll go."

His expression transformed for a brief second, his smile widening as he pulled the keys from the ignition. "Good."

She hadn't missed that look: a flash of elation before he'd glanced away. He was happy she'd said yes, and boy, that thrilled her way more than it should.

She swung her door open. "So are you going to tell me why we're here?"

He shook his head and reached into the back of the car. "First, you'll need these."

Odd. With a curious smile, she opened the paper bag he offered, then stuck her hand in.

She gasped, slowly pulling out a thick, A5-sized leather-bound journal, then a set of Derwent sketch pencils, followed by a box of top-quality HB leads.

"Matt," she breathed, taking in the wonderful smell of new paper and wood before refocusing on him. "You don't have to buy me stuff."

He shrugged but AJ could see the satisfaction in his smile. "There's more."

"What?"

"I'll show you."

AJ stood in front of Van Gogh's famous *Sunflowers* painting and let the beauty of the moment wash over her in stunned silence.

A private showing. For her. That was just... He was...

For the first time in her life, someone actually *got* her.

It was way too much.

She quickly blinked away a sudden well of tears, then took a deep breath while her heart kept on pounding.

"The Starry Night," she said softly, staring at the gorgeous

swirl of blue night sky scattered with yellow stars. "Oh, the self-portrait. *Irises.* Oh, wow, that's *Café Terrace at Night!*" She gave a small clap and surged forward until she was standing right in front of the painting, taking in the bold strokes and rainbow colors.

"I have a poster of this on my bedroom wall at home. This is amazing. How did you manage to pull this off?"

He shrugged. "I know people."

"Well, thank you *so* much."

"You're welcome."

She knew she was grinning like a crazy woman but she couldn't help it. Joy welled up, overwhelming her, propelling her forward.

A second later she wrapped her arms around his neck and hugged him.

His arms automatically went around her, pulling her deep into his warmth, and when she eased back, the kiss was inevitable. A breathless, hot kiss that AJ wasn't sure she'd initiated. Either way, she welcomed it, welcomed his mouth, his hands, his chest pressed up against hers. And when he finally broke away with a soft groan, her disappointment echoed his.

"Take your time," he said thickly, taking a step back and shoving his hands in his pockets. "We have two hours."

She nodded, unable to speak, then quickly turned to the journal she'd left on the leather lounge. She fumbled with the pencil box, but she finally managed to get one out. He'd not only bought her art supplies, but he'd also had the freaking art gallery open just for her.

Whoa, hold on a second. She suddenly panicked.

This was just Matt being thoughtful. She'd mentioned it days ago and he'd remembered. That was all. Yet she still couldn't stop a thread of delight spreading through her belly. Something that felt this good couldn't possibly be bad, right?

Right.

She pressed her lips together and opened the journal,

smoothed out the unlined pristine page and switched her focus to the amazing art before her.

The next few days passed in a blur, and by the time Saturday rolled around again, AJ felt like she was about to explode from the anticipation.

After the art gallery, they'd eaten a late dinner at the Quay, then he'd dropped her off at Zac's apartment. His gentle goodnight kiss seared her lips, and she'd practically floated to the top floor.

The routine was set for the next few days: Matt would call in the morning to let her know what time he'd be by, then when the time rolled around, he'd pick her up and they'd go out to dinner. AJ asked about his travels and his job, listening with single-minded attention, determined not to stare at his mouth, those expressive hands. A couple of times she must've lapsed because he'd suddenly stop midsentence and give her such a heated look that it made her skin go all prickly.

The first few days they'd been the picture of restraint. He'd taken her back to Zac's apartment, kissed her on the cheek and left. But after the third night, his patience had obviously worn thin. She'd turned to say good-night and found herself caught up in a rush of lips, eager fingers and panting breath. When Matt finally stepped back with a groan, his frustrated expression echoed her own.

"A suggestion, not an unbreakable rule," AJ muttered in the cool silence now, staring at the shadowed bedroom ceiling. Dr. Adams had confirmed it today. She was due for her first procedure in two weeks' time and a lapse beforehand certainly wouldn't ruin her chances.

So what was the problem?

With a grunt, she rolled over on her side and punched the pillow.

She liked spending time with him. Liked holding his hand. Liked ending the evening with a kiss that left her wanting more. This time, their relationship wasn't just about sex, even if the desperate need for it was killing her.

And he hadn't pushed.

Now here she was, about to spend a week with him, and suddenly all she could think about was his slow smile as he pushed her hair behind one ear. His warm mouth as he kissed her.

"Damn it!" She groaned and pressed her thighs together.

Five days. It'd probably kill her. And after her first procedure, her opportunities to make love would be zero.

She sighed. She'd drawn a line and unless she crossed it herself, she was pretty sure Matt wouldn't.

It was up to her.

They boarded the plane an hour before takeoff. AJ was introduced to Carly, Matt's assistant, then his head of security, James Decker, a brash American dressed all in black with a charming grin and biceps the size of an off-season bodybuilder's.

"Nice to meet you, AJ," he said before glancing past her to his boss. "So…" He waggled a finger between her and Matt. "How'd you two meet?"

"I—"

"We need to board so the pilot can do his checks," Matt interrupted, picking up AJ's suitcase. "You have everything?"

Decker's grin lingered. "*I* do. Do you?"

"Yep."

A cold wind screamed over the tarmac, and AJ shoved her hands deep in her pockets. There was subtext there, but she couldn't work out exactly what.

"So let's go." Matt nodded for her to head up the steps first and she eagerly ascended, the brand-new Australian passport burning a hole in her jeans pocket.

Whatever she was expecting was nothing compared to the reality of Faro. Bustling, colorful Faro with its outdoor markets, cobblestoned streets and friendly locals. Sure, the five-star eighteenth-century Monte Do Casal country house with its pristine walls, sparkling pool and expansive gardens had all sorts of indulgent offerings, from poolside service to massages and facials. But she was more interested in what was going on outside, eager to experience the sights and sounds and smells of the town. Dressed in a loose knee-length skirt and tank top, she managed to secure a table at a café on a busy main road and spent a few hours sketching before she decided to explore.

Discovering a new city alone was a familiar routine, one she'd done since she was seventeen. Yet as she wandered the streets, soaking up every little detail, a niggling thought struck. *Matt should be here to see this.*

She paused at a bodega, peering into the smoky darkness with a frown. That was silly—he'd probably seen this city a dozen times before. Probably not alone, either. Her frown deepened, only to freeze a second later.

Was she jealous? But she wasn't the jealous type. Because that would mean...

"*Senhorita* would like to see our pretty gold rings?"

Her train of thought broken by the swarthy street vendor, she politely declined, shaking her head with an apologetic smile.

No. Getting attached was not part of the plan.

Not ever.

On the second day Matt declared his business concluded, gave Decker and Carly the rest of the week off and they moved out of their hotel.

They drove out of the city in a hired car and headed west on the A25 toward Lagos. The road hugged the coastline, and the view was nothing short of spectacular, with sheer cliff faces, sparkling blue water and lush vegetation. AJ practically hung out the window, engrossed in the breathless beauty of it all.

They got to Lagos in less than two hours. To her surprise,

Matt had booked them into a *pensione* instead of a flashy hotel. They took the top floor while the owners occupied the ground level.

The house was clean, with a private bathroom and a balcony with stunning rooftop views and a view of the main marketplace a couple of streets away. And just like the expensive Faro hotel, it had separate beds.

When AJ saw this, she was both relieved and disappointed. He'd booked both places and couldn't have sent a clearer message than separate beds.

Matt hired a motorbike and they spent the next four days sightseeing. They drove up into the mountains to a small church high in the hills. They explored the street sellers, visited the local Lagos museum. On their fourth day, they spent hours on the beach in comfortable silence, where she sketched the glorious sunset while he lazed on a blanket next to her. When the light finally waned, she glanced up to find him studying her so intensely that her mouth suddenly went dry.

The streetlights flickered on, casting them in a hazy glow as AJ slowly replaced her pencils in her case and snapped the lid shut with a sigh. "That's it. Light's gone."

Matt nodded and stood, brushing off his pants, then offering his hand. Without hesitation she took it, and his warm fingers wrapped around hers, an intimacy that never failed to make her blood quicken.

"Angel…"

"Hmm?" She looked up, waiting, but he said nothing, just devoured her with those dark eyes until finally he glanced away.

"We should go and eat. Our flight's early and you still haven't packed."

When they got back to the *pensione,* she changed into a strapless white cotton dress with buttons from neck to the knee-length hem. She paired it with an azure cardigan, knowing the color made her eyes pop. Her hair was up this time, casually messy and drawn back at the nape. A pair of dangly blue stones—a birthday present from Emily—hung from her ears and her butterfly necklace rested at her throat.

From the look in Matt's eyes, she'd made the right choice.

He offered his hand and she automatically took it, taking pleasure in that small contact as they walked to a restaurant on the corner. The place was decorated as a rustic street, with cobbled floors, skillfully painted stone hacienda walls and overarching olive trees in huge earthenware pots. Tables were scattered throughout, circular booths ringed the outer edges, and at the far end, a fully stocked bar was seeing a brisk trade.

They were led to a secluded booth, their only light two candles on the table. She slid in first and Matt followed until they were hip to hip. His warmth scorched her thigh, and despite her hunger, she wanted nothing more than to touch him, run her fingers over that long smooth forearm, knead the muscle beneath his skin.

"Does the butterfly mean something?"

She blinked. "Hmm?"

"Your necklace." Her hand went to the pendant. "You always wear it. Is it special?"

"Yes." She stroked the edge of one wing with her finger. "Emily gave it to me for my thirtieth birthday." She paused. "It means reinvention. Regeneration."

"The metamorphosis from caterpillar to butterfly."

She nodded.

"I like it." He reached out and gently ran his thumb over the mother-of-pearl wings. "Did you reinvent yourself often?"

"A few times. I—" She stopped.

"Let me guess," he said softly, finally releasing the necklace. "Your past is off-limits, right?"

She nodded, feeling foolish even though she knew that wasn't Matt's intention.

Tell him.

She glanced away, skin prickling under his silent scrutiny. "My mother was sixteen and pregnant with me when she was kicked out of her home. We lived off welfare until she hooked up with my stepfather, a delightful man who got her addicted to booze and drugs." She stopped, face flaming. *Too much. Way too much.* Yet something in his face, in that open, non-judgmental expression, made her forge on. "Parents are supposed to look after their kids, not make them lie and steal and dread every knock on the door. But we survived." She managed a shaky smile. "Well, I guess Emily's doing better than just surviving. She always was the big believer in the glorious fairy-tale of love."

He arched an eyebrow. "You don't believe in love?"

"Of course I do. Just not the whole Prince-Charming-riding-in-to-sweep-me-off-my-feet thing." When he remained silent, she added a little defiantly, "I spent a lot of years on my own. It tend to makes you a realist."

He studied her for an age, almost as if he were waiting for something more. She met his scrutiny head-on, and as the seconds passed, an uncomfortable panic began to leech in. "Don't look at me like that."

"Like what?"

"Like you're sad for me. I don't need it. I don't—" *Need you.* No, that felt wrong and she managed to stop the words before they formed.

She heard him sigh and the mood suddenly changed. "Look, AJ, I understand your need for control, I really do. But closing yourself off to possibilities isn't the right way to go about it."

She scowled and leaned back in the seat. "Why are we even talking about this again?"

"Because talking is what people do."

She huffed out a breath. "I knew this would happen. I'd mention my past and you'd…"

"I'd what?" Matt's expression was a mix of sadness and understanding. Not disgust. Not pity. Yet somehow, his sympathy did something to her insides and she had to glance away. "You can let your past define you, let it keep chipping away at who you are, or you can make a decision and take control."

"Like you did after your brother's accident?"

His mouth tightened for one second. "Yeah."

AJ flushed and clamped her mouth shut. Where on earth had that cheap shot come from? Yet as she studied him, she sensed something behind that smooth expression. What would it take to relieve him of that burden?

More than she could offer. Certainly nothing she could say because hadn't she already stuck her foot in it?

So instead, she placed a hand over his, leaned in and kissed him.

It was a gentle kiss, devoid of ulterior motive. It wasn't a precursor to passion. It was a kiss with the full brunt of her emotional state behind it, and for one second she felt him go still beneath her mouth, almost as if she'd shocked him and he was unsure of what to do.

She let her eyes close, moving slowly, testing the swell of his full bottom lip between hers. His sigh, when it came, shuddered into her and that's when she knew she'd done the right thing.

They kissed for ages, leisurely exploring each other in the dim restaurant light, pressed together from shoulder to thigh. When they finally broke apart, Matt glanced down at the table, then laughed.

AJ followed his gaze. While they'd been lip locked, their waiter had discreetly left their meals, topped up their glasses and added some cutlery.

"This place has excellent service," AJ got out.

Matt nodded, his smile matching hers. "I agree."

By unspoken agreement, they sought each other again, but this time AJ felt the urgency behind his kiss. The pressure had changed, going from sweet to insistent. Then his hand slipped under the table to gently rest on her knee.

She momentarily broke the kiss. "Matt?"

"Mmm?" His hand left her knee, stroking as it eased higher to her thigh.

"We can't."

"Why not?"

Her head swam. *Why not indeed?* "For starters, we're in a public place."

"So we are." AJ felt a tremor of excitement as his fingers crept under the hem of her dress, making their way teasingly up. She held her breath, desperate to see how far he would actually go before one of them put a stop to it.

Would she? Would he?

And still his hand went higher.

She met his gaze and held it. He was at her inner thigh now, his fingers creating a warm path ever upward. Then...

She held her breath as he gently stroked her through the thin cotton of her knickers.

"Matt..."

Slowly, regretfully it seemed, he withdrew. "You don't think we should do this." Her nod, when it came, was a little too reluctant. "But do you *want* to?"

She clamped off a groan and murmured something under her breath.

"What?"

She shook her head. "Let's just eat, okay?"

He stared at her for the longest time, until her eyes darted away to her plate. With infinite care, she silently drew it across the table, picked up her fork then proceeded to eat.

"Fine, Angel. We'll eat."

Thirteen

They walked back to the *pensione,* only this time he didn't take her hand, and it made AJ's heart ache.

No, it was bigger than that. Everything inside ached, like someone had come along and stolen a vital part of herself, and that loss only exacerbated the chaos.

"Matt?"

"Yeah?" He pushed the front door open and let her go in first. She mounted the narrow staircase, more than aware of his presence close behind. When they reached the top of the stairs, she turned to face him. "Back at the beach. You were going to ask me something but didn't." His brows dipped but he said nothing. "What was it?"

"Nothing."

He made a move to go past her but she grabbed his arm, forcing him to stop. "Just say it. I want to know."

He huffed out a sigh. "I was going to ask you about the night we broke up."

She dropped his arm and took a step back. "Why do you want to talk about that?"

"How long did it take for you to forgive me?"

"I just—" Wow, what could she say to that? "I didn't blame you." It was true. She'd blamed herself.

"Not even after the way I just dropped it on you?"

"No." She turned and walked down the short corridor toward their bedroom door. Matt followed. "Why are you asking now? The past is past. Going over it won't change anything."

She shoved the door open, went straight to the wardrobe and grabbed her suitcase.

"You don't like talking about the past, do you?"

She snapped her gaze up, irritated by his brusqueness. "Just because I don't blurt out every tiny detail about my life doesn't mean it's wrong." She turned to the bureau, grabbed a handful of underwear and tossed them into the open case.

"I'm not saying that. But you need to give a little, AJ. You can't expect someone to open up to you if you don't do the same."

I don't want to open up. Not to you. "This isn't part of our deal, Matt," she said softly.

He studied her in cool silence before saying, "That night we broke up? I'd just come off a twelve-hour shift. My tardiness and distraction hadn't gone unnoticed those past six months. I'd had 'the talk' from my parents, then my senior resident—"

"Matt…"

"And the second time, I had to step up and make a choice."

She glared at him as he tried to make his point. *The teeny, tiny point.* "Your career came first." When it came, his slow nod only confirmed what she'd thought all along. "And I wasn't Matthew Cooper girlfriend material."

"I didn't say that."

"You didn't need to. You never once introduced me to your family or took me out where someone from your social circle might see us. Or…or…even invited me to your Christmas party," she added tightly.

If he'd really wanted her, he would've found a way to work it out, right? AJ thought.

He gave a short, exasperated sigh. "I thought you were okay with things being casual. I didn't know you wanted to—"

"Well, you never asked!" Her hands went to her hips, irritation surging through her.

He mirrored her stance. "Nor did you!"

She stood there in silence until she couldn't take it anymore. "Fine. You want to know? I'll tell you. I was planning on staying in town and I was trying to work out the best way to tell you."

The shock on his face was almost laughable. Almost. But instead of laughter, a deep burning embarrassment welled up in her throat, scalding her neck, then her cheeks.

"AJ..."

"Please don't, Matt." She whirled and grabbed a dress from the wardrobe, folding it with sharp precision. "It was a long time ago. I got over it." *Oh, you are such a liar.* "I moved on. So let's just—"

The shrill sound of a phone splintered the air and with a soft curse, Matt whirled and grabbed the offending gadget from the dresser.

"Yes, Mum?"

All the fight drained from AJ with those two little words and she left him to his call, walking into the bathroom to gather her toiletries. As she packed her shampoo, conditioner, toothbrush and toothpaste, she couldn't shake the ominous feeling that she'd put her foot right in it.

You're smarter than this.

She couldn't change the past and there was no point arguing with Matt about it. He didn't need to know how much that rejection had hurt, how it had shaped every relationship since him.

The past had no bearing on the here and now. They both understood this was a physical arrangement, not a romantic one. God, what would he do if he knew she'd been fantasizing about their relationship these past few weeks? That sometimes, in the lonely early-morning light when she imagined them being a real couple, it made everything ache like she'd already lost something she'd never get back?

She was so caught up in her turbulent thoughts she didn't realize he was standing in the doorway until she caught his reflection in the mirror.

He was staring at her with an odd, intense look, as if he

wanted to say something yet wasn't sure she'd want to hear it. A look so unlike Matt that it gave her pause.

She took a deep breath and turned around. "Look, this is stupid, us arguing. I made some silly choices the past ten years." Not to mention reckless and downright dangerous ones, too. She'd been crazy, eager to push boundaries, eager to forget. "But they were *my* choices, and I don't regret them." She'd also learned some hard lessons about life and love and for that she'd always be grateful. "You also made a choice and did what you thought was right. Let's just drop it, shall we?"

She hated it when he said nothing. His scrutiny was so focused, as if he was trying to figure out all the dark marks on her heart. "My parents have some spare tickets for a benefit on Tuesday. Do you want to come with me?"

She frowned. "What?"

"You, me, a Saint Cat's fund-raiser. Will you be my date?"

Yes! No! No, wait…

Confusion warred inside her, her resolution to keep Matt at a distance battling with other, deeper desires. "I don't think that's a good idea."

"Why not?"

Her hands went to her hips. "Oh, only about a dozen reasons. Me and your parents, for one."

"They don't bite."

She snorted. "That's not what I meant. You're the one who still has to work with the hospital."

"It's the twenty-first century, AJ. We're allowed to go out in public without a chaperone."

"Don't be obtuse. You know what I mean."

"Oh, I'm sure they're already talking about us." He crossed his arms and fixed her with a direct look. "We went to see Saint Cat's top fertility specialist together. Our names are on forms, computer systems and now tests. You can't keep secrets in a hospital for long."

Of course, he was right. It didn't matter to her, but… "Does it bother you? The fact that people are probably talking about you?"

He shrugged. "They've been doing that all my life."

"I see."

A beat passed. "So you never did answer. Are you afraid of being seen with me?"

"No." She turned and shoved her moisturizer into her toiletries bag.

He stepped inside the bathroom and crossed his arms, eyes glinting as he blocked her exit. She glared back and let her unimpressed expression do all the talking.

He wasn't buying it. "I don't believe it. AJ Reynolds is *afraid* of meeting my parents?"

"Now, listen here—"

"That's just not possible." He advanced slowly, his mouth slanted into a mocking grin. "Not the same woman who shared my bed last week."

No, don't talk about that! "Matt—" She backed up into the vanity, her butt resting on the cool marble as her heart quickened.

"Not the same AJ who kissed me so hard I couldn't breathe." His hands went out, trapping her against the vanity as he leaned in. "The same one who squirmed beneath me," he whispered. "Writhing and panting as I kissed every inch of her skin—"

AJ's eyes drifted closed, the hot memory washing over her, bathing her in desire. A second later his lips went to her neck and she sighed, welcoming, wanting.

"—then demanded I take her hard and fast on my office desk."

Her hands went to his nape and she dragged his mouth to hers with a soft groan. Yet he held back, the muscles in his neck straining under her grip, eyes liquid pools of chocolate. "What are you afraid of, Angel?"

"Nothing." *Everything. You. Me. This.*

"Then come with me."

How much had she wanted this all those years ago? To be
the one on his arm, introduced and included in his life. And
now the desperate need flared in her yet again. She wanted to
see what his life had been like without her, what had shaped
him, who he'd been. A life she regretted not fighting harder to
be involved with in the first place, if she were brutally honest.

She breathed out slowly. "Okay."

God, that smile. That brilliant, triumphant smile that
wounded her so low and deep. He undid her a thousand times
over.

Then his mouth swooped down to cover hers.

AJ could never get enough of his kisses, the way he took
control, devouring her. The way his breath filled her mouth
and her senses, his soft murmurs cranking her desire into a
long, slow burn of need.

He swiftly grabbed her bottom, hiking her up onto the
vanity, and she wrapped her legs around his waist, urging
him closer.

Their week of abstinence was over. He wanted her. And
she wanted him right back.

"Matt…" she gasped against his lips. "We…"

"Do you trust me?"

A low groan reverberated in her throat. She loved the way
his dark eyes went languid with passion. They bore into her,
as if she was his sole focus and he had no place else he'd
rather be.

"Do you trust me?" he repeated.

Her heart twisted. "Yes."

"Then we can do this."

"It won't ruin anything?"

"I promise. I'm a doctor, remember?"

She swallowed. Her body felt like it was on fire, so desperate was her need, and it took barely a second to make the
decision. She nodded, not trusting herself to speak.

Everything happened in a split second—the frenzy of
clothes being shoved up, off or aside. Her legs spreading at

his touch, her mouth parting beneath his eager tongue. The hiss of excitement when skin met skin, then an excruciating pause as Matt readied himself.

Then one hard, swift plunge and they were engulfed in the scorching, familiar heat, their cries of delight echoing through the bathroom.

Matt pounded into her, his hard thrusts skidding her across the cold marble as his fingers dug into her bottom. She groaned and crossed her ankles so her heels bumped on the delicious curve where his lower back met his butt. He was deep, so very deep and it felt so very right.

"Yes," she murmured, urging him on. He filled her completely, his thick length sliding intimately in, out, in, out, his tongue an erotic echo in her mouth. They tangled, they battled, they took. And they shared, too—from breath and kisses to the slick, damp heat intimately joining them in a familiar dance.

AJ climaxed and threw her head back with a cry, losing herself to the bursts of light behind her eyelids. She felt Matt spill into her, his deep groan of satisfaction echoing as everything inside contracted and shuddered.

"Matt..." she breathed. "I..."

He cut her off with a kiss, his mouth gently searing hers. A tender, almost loving gesture that squeezed at something deep inside, something she'd thought buried long ago, prickling her eyes and sending every sense into meltdown.

She broke off the kiss to lay her cheek against his shoulder, her heartbeat filling every slow second.

She squeezed her eyes shut. They had history and chemistry. That was it. That was all it could ever be.

She would not fall in love with Matthew Cooper because that would be supremely stupid. And she, AJ Reynolds, was not stupid.

By nine the next morning they were miles above the earth, on their way back to Sydney. Matt glanced over at AJ, nose-deep in a book, then to Decker, stretched out and asleep behind his dark sunglasses, then to Carly, who was single-mindedly tapping away on her laptop.

He sighed and returned to the schedule laid out on his iPad, but moments later he gave up.

AJ had opened up, stunning him with that little truth from her past.

She'd been planning to stay. How could he have not seen that? But he'd been blind to anything but his own problems and gotten in first, shot her down, and she'd left.

He rubbed the bridge of his nose and scowled.

Now here they were again, treading familiar ground, coming together and getting lost in that crazy desire just like before. *No, not like before.* His eyes darted to her bright red hair, the gentle curve of her cheek. He knew what he wanted now. And AJ...well, she wanted something, too. And apparently that didn't include him.

He'd felt her withdrawal this morning, the way she didn't meet his eyes, the subtle wall she put between them. He'd reassured her that their lovemaking hadn't stuffed anything up but wasn't entirely sure she believed him.

He cast his mind back to the previous night, and suddenly everything flooded in: AJ writhing beneath him, calling his name as he drove deep inside, loving her until they finally collapsed, sated and spent. And later, in bed, she'd driven him crazy with her hands and body, her shock of hair as it teased his sensitive nipples, brushed over his belly, then lower when she took him in her mouth with bold delight.

Damn. He shifted in his seat, trying to relieve the sudden tightness in his groin. Despite that incredible chemistry, he still had no idea what was going on in her head. Oh, she'd let down her guard a little, allowing a brief glimpse inside, but it still wounded him, the way she'd so grudgingly shared that snippet.

Yeah, and you're an open book, right?

AJ glanced up then, meeting his eyes, and he realized he'd been staring.

She blinked, her bright eyes assessing, searching, a hesitant smile hovering on her lips. That tiny uncertainty—from a woman so very sure of everything else in her life—tore at his heart.

He'd put that uncertainty there and he had a lot to make up for. So he held her gaze and put everything he had into his smile, every remembered kiss, every touch, every breath they'd shared.

Her eyes widened…and then there it was, the lush curve of her mouth, the seductive crease of her cat's eyes before she ducked her head and returned to her book.

There was his Angel.

And just like that, he fell. Totally, completely.

He loved her. Loved everything about her—all those doubts, all those tiny scars on her heart, her fractured past that had shaped her into the strong, independent woman she was now.

But would it be enough? Would *he* be enough?

There was only one way to find out. He had to keep going forward.

AJ refused to let disappointment show when Matt dropped her off at Zac's apartment. Instead, she pasted on a smile and accepted his kiss on the cheek.

"I have to go to work," he murmured, his lips lingering, giving her goose bumps. "I have a meeting tonight."

"On a Sunday?"

"Conference call. I'll call you, okay?"

"Sure."

She watched him go, her gaze drinking in his long stride, the way the expensive suit sat on his lean frame, the shaggy hairline that brushed his collar.

She whirled to the elevator, forcing back inexplicable tears. Lust had never gripped her so surely before, trapping her in tight claws until he was all she could think about.

She furiously pressed the up button over and over, determined to ignore the way her breath hitched. And what of last night? How would that affect her chances of getting pregnant? Surely it had consequences, despite his reassurances.

The elevator doors slid open and she strode in, dumping her bag on the floor before digging out her phone and dialing Dr. Adams's number.

As much as she wanted Matt, burned for him like a bush-fire had taken up residence under her skin, she couldn't jeopardize her chances. She had to know the facts. And if that meant complete abstinence, then so be it.

Ten minutes later, after Dr. Adams had eased her mind, she ran a bath, cranked up her iPod and turned her attention to the novel she'd been trying to read since the flight. But she only managed a few pages before restlessness got the better of her.

"Damn you, Matthew Cooper," she muttered, rising from the water and grabbing a towel. After making herself a cup of tea, she pulled out her sketch pad and pencils and began to work.

Fourteen

It was the night of the hospital benefit and AJ was, quite frankly, scared.

Matt's compliments had briefly warmed her—she'd chosen a red below-the-knee ruffled dress with a tight corset bodice—but trepidation had set in as they drove to the Pullman Quay Grand at Sydney Harbour.

If Matt noticed, he didn't say anything. They parked, then made their way into the fancy foyer, all massive windows and panoramic views of the harbor. AJ barely had time to take it all in before he was guiding her toward the restaurant where a bunch of perfectly dressed people were milling about.

This was it. She was actually doing this. With a deep breath, she straightened, pulling her shoulders back.

"You okay?"

She glanced up at him, at the concern creasing his brow. "Yes, I just…" She paused then said carefully, "I don't like crowds."

"Really?"

"They make me nervous, all those people watching," she lied. Truth was, she'd been assessed, dissected and judged before and it had stopped worrying her a long time ago. No, it was the parent thing that freaked her out. She didn't do parents. They made her nervous.

He eyed the packed gathering inside the restaurant, wall-to-wall people in their designer dresses and suits, the loud murmur of voices, clinking glasses and occasional laughter spilling out, then he turned to her with a reassuring smile.

"Honestly, I don't think they'll notice us."

"Matthew! You're late!"

A woman emerged from the crowd and made her way toward them. She was tall, regal and flawlessly done up in a black shift dress and kitten heels. The family resemblance was obvious.

AJ swallowed as she watched Matt's mother kiss his cheek, then slowly turn to her.

"Hello, I'm Dr. Alicia Cooper." The hand she offered was cool and smooth and AJ shook it with a vague feeling of inadequacy, well aware of every mark and freckle on her own.

Still, she managed a polite smile and greeting.

"Matthew, you know Mason Palmer, chief of oncology?" She swept her hand to the man who had stepped up beside her, a tall, good-looking guy in an impeccable suit. They ran through the mandatory introductions before Alicia turned back to AJ. "So, how do you know Matthew?"

"We're…ah…" She glanced at Matt, then back to Alicia's sharp scrutiny. "Old friends. We go back a long way."

"Really. And what do you do?" Alicia efficiently looked AJ up and down before giving her a polite smile. She was being judged—and probably found lacking—behind that cool, elegant charm.

AJ tipped her chin and stared right back at her. "I'm an artist."

"How interesting. What medium do you use?"

"Watercolor mostly." She glanced over at Alicia's companion, who was looking exceedingly bored with the whole interaction.

"I see. Well, don't monopolize each other all night," she said with a smile. A perfectly fine smile except for the irritation behind it, AJ thought. "Lots of people are here—influential people," she added with a pointed look at Matt. "Make sure you mingle. Have a lovely time."

"We will." AJ returned her smile and, for added effect, looped her arm through Matt's. With another icy smile, Alicia Cooper moved on.

After a moment, AJ slowly slipped her arm from Matt's and stared into the crowd in silence.

"Sorry."

"What for?"

"My mother can be somewhat…abrasive."

"She was perfectly fine."

"Right." He scanned the crowd and muttered something under his breath.

AJ leaned in. "Sorry?"

"I said, I'd rather be at home than at this excruciating party, making small talk and being judged."

Oh. She stared at him. Was it wrong that she was thinking exactly the same thing? And should she even admit that? What would it mean if she did? And—

"Angel." He leaned in, his lips close to her ear. "You creep me out when you're so silent. Just say what's on your mind."

But all she could do was shake her head. It would benefit no one to give voice to the strange longing she'd felt ever since they'd returned from Portugal. Their time together had an expiration date. He had an insanely busy career; that had been painfully clear these past few weeks. They'd even signed an agreement, for heaven's sake. It would do absolutely no good to start wishing for something different.

She wouldn't. She *couldn't.*

"I'm going to the bathroom," she muttered, turning from his loaded gaze before she said something completely stupid and ruined all her careful plans.

She was leaning against her closed stall door, giving herself a little pep talk, when she heard two women come in.

"Did you see Matt's date?"

AJ froze.

"Oh, yes, I've met her." That was Katrina. "Pleasant enough. A bit too…brassy, though."

AJ's mouth dropped into an outraged O. *Brassy*?

"Do you think it's natural?" the other woman went on. .

"Looks like it. God knows why you'd want to keep that color, though."

"She's got an arse on her, too."

They both laughed as AJ scowled at the stall door, her anger practically burning a hole in the wood.

"She's obviously punching above her weight," the other woman added. "I mean, look at Matt—rich, gorgeous, talented. It won't last."

Then she heard the door swing open and a new voice declare, "Hi, Katrina. Who are we talking about?"

"Matthew's redhead."

"AJ?" AJ held her breath. The new arrival was Matt's sister, Paige. "Oh, we met her at her sister's wedding—Zac and Emily Prescott? She's perfectly lovely."

"Really."

"Yes." There was a pause, then a hushed whisper. Then, suddenly, thundering silence.

AJ had been in the stall long enough. And the others had obviously worked that out, too. With a sigh, she flushed, pulled her shoulders back, then swung the door open.

Her eyes met Paige's first in the mirror, and the woman gave her a genuine smile as she smoothed back her sleek dark hair. As the ominous silence lengthened, AJ offered a nod and a slightly dimmer smile to Katrina and her cohort, then proceeded to wash and dry her hands.

"I love your hairstyle, AJ," Paige said, flicking a deliberate glance at Katrina. "Very Rita Hayworth."

"Thanks." AJ smoothed the curls around her fingers and let them spring back.

She turned to go, then very slowly glanced back to Katrina. "Oh, by the way, Katrina—if you *are* going to talk about someone, make sure the stalls are empty before you do.

Otherwise you'll come across as a gossipy bitch. Not a good look for the hospital, I should think." She speared her companion with a look. "And for the record—Matt and I are just using each other for sex."

With that hanging in the air, AJ pushed the bathroom door open and made a dignified exit.

This was temporary. So why was she so upset? Face burning, she stalked down the tiled corridor back to the party. Matt was in her bed—albeit briefly—not in her life.

Stupid. *He's been your entire life only for the past...* She mentally calculated. Three weeks. They'd shared a bed, numerous meals. And yes, she'd gradually revealed tiny pieces of her life, stuff no one besides Emily knew. And sometimes, even stuff her sister didn't know.

This was ridiculous. She was comfortable in her skin and all too aware of the world around her. She normally shrugged off negative comments and rude attitudes when she encountered them. So why had that bitch session back there gotten under her skin?

She had no idea. But damn, it hurt.

"AJ! Wait!"

She turned and spotted Paige. Matt's sister snagged two glasses of champagne from a passing waiter, then caught up with her.

"I don't drink." AJ gently shook her head at the proffered glass.

"Oh, well." Paige shrugged, then downed half a glass in a few gulps. She grinned at AJ, finished it off, then shoved the empty glass on another passing waiter's tray.

AJ said nothing, just studied Matt's sister in silence. She was tall and lean, with big brown eyes and dark hair pinned back with a diamante Kylie band. Paige was a female version of Matt, dressed in a seventies-style tunic dress tied with a thin belt and accessorized by a heap of silver chains with dangly charms.

"So you're seeing my brother," she began, tipping the second glass to her lips.

"Not really."

Paige's eyes creased in thoughtful scrutiny. "That's not what I hear."

AJ shrugged. "I don't listen to gossip."

"Oh, everyone *listens*." Paige tapped her be-ringed finger against the glass. "Doesn't mean you have to pay attention to it. For instance, I also heard Matt took you to Portugal on a job."

When AJ remained silent, Paige smiled. "Diplomatic silence—that's good. I like you already." Then she shocked AJ by linking her arm through hers with a bright smile. "And anyone who can ruffle Katrina's feathers is okay by me. Let's have a chat."

From his vantage point near the bar, Matt had a perfect view of the restaurant. He glanced past the pristine tables, the mingling guests working out their seating arrangements, to the rest of the crowd milling around the bar and the glorious view of the harbor sunset. Still no sign of her shock of red hair or her fire engine–red dress.

He waved off a passing waiter as he continued his search. When he finally found AJ at the far end of the room, deep in conversation with Paige, he frowned. His sister was incredibly nosy, incredibly determined and a hopeless romantic. She also had a tendency to grill his dates and weed out at least one flaw, no matter how deeply it was buried.

What would she find with AJ?

As he contemplated going over there, he felt someone come up behind him.

"So you brought your date from Maxfield with you?"

He glanced over his shoulder at Katrina. She wore a sleek, sleeveless green gown, her eyebrows raised.

"Yes."

"That was weeks ago."

"Yep."

She followed his gaze, eyes narrowed as she studied AJ more closely. "Pretty enough, I suppose. In a brassy, wild kind of way."

"Careful, Katrina. Your inner bitch is showing."

Her brows ratcheted higher. "And you are acting oddly devoted to one woman."

He said nothing.

"So, I heard some interesting gossip about you visiting Sandi the other week."

He schooled his expression into casual blankness. He didn't have to explain himself to anyone, especially not Katrina. Yet behind the intrusive question and her cool study, he detected a genuine interest. He'd been married to the woman for eight years and no matter how it had ended, they'd still been through a lot. He let a small breath go. "We're trying for a baby, yes."

For one second Matt thought he detected something flash behind Katrina's cool green eyes before she said drily, "Well, good for you."

"Thanks."

They both glanced back to AJ, still in conversation with Paige.

"Your sister seems to like her."

"Looks like," Matt said neutrally. Paige had hated Katrina and they both knew it.

"Well, I'll leave you to it." She placed a hand on his arm. "Enjoy the night, Matt." Then she leaned in, deposited a kiss on his cheek and said softly, "Be happy."

In stunned silence he watched her go, her long, tanned frame cutting a striking figure as she confidently made her way through the crowd.

Wow. That was odd. Totally out of character.

When a waiter offered him a drink, he took it, taking a swig without tasting it.

Be happy.

He was trying.

* * *

Paige had moved off to get another drink, leaving AJ temporarily alone. With a glass of ice water in her hands, she casually scanned the room, noting everything and everyone with a keen eye before moving on.

Ahh. Right there. Her insides did a little dance. He was so tall and lean, whatever he wore always looked good. But Matt in a suit was truly devastating. The charcoal suit, white shirt and tie were a perfect foil to his shaggy hair and stubble. An intriguing mix of bohemian and professional, a look she knew was entirely accidental on his part.

He was watching someone or something and she followed his gaze across the room to where a familiar figure stood in conversation with a handful of people.

Katrina.

She looked away, but the damage was already done. Bitter and unwanted jealousy rattled her composure, leaving her angry and frustrated.

Sure, Matt had a past, but so did she. It was stupid to be angry.

She took a chug of water then palmed the damp base of the glass. Yeah, if you looked at it *logically*. But when she was around Matt, logic just flew out the window.

"Hey, AJ, come and meet some people."

She squared her shoulders, sighed and turned to a smiling Paige. "Sure."

So for the next few hours, AJ threw herself into perfect date mode, smiling, making small talk and generally charming the pants off everyone she met. An aching face and sore feet were a small price to pay because when they finally left, Matthew's satisfied smile made her glow.

"Did you have a good time?" he asked as they waited for the valet to bring his car around.

She nodded. "I really like your sister."

"Yeah, you two chatted for ages."

AJ nodded. "We made a date for the Powerhouse next week.

The Harry Potter exhibit," she added, eyeing the sleek Jaguar as it emerged from the underground parking lot.

"She asked you to go with her?"

She glanced up at him. Had she crossed a line? "I can cancel if you think it's not—"

"No, no." He nodded to the valet, then eased into the car. AJ followed, closing the door softly behind her. "I'm just surprised. Paige's never liked anyone I went out with."

"No one? Not even Katrina?"

"Especially not Katrina."

That confirmed it then. AJ's estimation of Paige Cooper increased a notch.

They drove down the road, both buried in silent thoughts as the thin traffic streamed around them.

Paige Cooper had been refreshingly, painfully forthcoming about the Cooper family, and once AJ had gotten over the shock, she'd been hooked. By the end of their conversation, AJ had been battling serious tears.

"Matt..."

"Yeah?"

She stared out the windshield at the car headlights and the brightly lit road as they made their way toward the Harbour Bridge. She contemplated her next words all the way across the bridge, down York Street and through Sydney's central business district.

It was only when they pulled up to her apartment that she finally settled on what to say.

"I know about Jack."

Oh, how quickly those shutters came down. *Remind you of someone?* "What do you know?"

"I know he was conceived so he could save your life." He frowned and cursed under his breath, but she ignored it. "That must've been tough."

He returned his gaze to the road, his knuckles flexing as he gripped the steering wheel. "Jack struggled with it for years."

"I meant for you."

He said nothing, just tightened his jaw.

"You were the favorite," she added.

He flushed. "I wasn't—"

"Yes, you were—are," she countered gently. "I only had to see your parents tonight to see it. The firstborn, the child genius, the youngest ever to graduate from UTS, the talented intern. And you had a baby brother whose entire existence was meant to save you."

He blinked slowly, his focus still out the window. "Jack called himself a 'harvest baby.' He…" He trailed off, blinked again.

"That's a lot to carry."

"He never really came to terms with the whole 'savior sibling' thing."

"Again, I meant for you."

AJ's heart ached as she watched his silent struggle, until his stormy eyes met hers, betraying the too-calm expression. "Jack had been living with Paige in London since he was seventeen. I'd only seen him once or twice before he died on that mountain."

Alarmed, she put a hand on his arm. "Oh, I didn't mean you should tell me—"

"No, I want to." He took a shuddering breath and seemed to draw strength in, as if he was letting something go in the retelling. "Since I can remember, my career has been carefully planned. Of course I would be a doctor, just like my mother and father, just like their parents and their parents before them. No other choice was considered. It motivated and drove my mum and dad, consuming everyone's lives." His mouth twisted briefly. "It didn't matter that Paige was an incredibly talented artist or that Jack had a way with animals. I was the important one. The Coopers have a lineage; our ancestors had titles and land and commanded power and respect. We're also academic high achievers and I was expected to be no different."

AJ nodded calmly.

"I was six years older than Jack but it felt like twenty. And my insane hours left no time for a life, let alone a baby brother who'd been told he was my only compatible donor, the reason I lived, ever since he could talk."

He paused suddenly, and AJ waited, her heart aching for him.

"After he died I lost it," he said quietly, hands tight on the wheel and his face half covered in shadow. "I escaped to a remote monastery in the Tibetan mountains, a place they opened up to Westerners only once a year for twenty days. The monks left me in peace for five days, even though I could hear them whispering behind the door. Then the priest put me to work assisting the goat herder." He paused, studying his knuckles. Then he slowly released the steering wheel and smiled. "You would've loved it. Think sweeping snow-topped mountains, vast green pastures, craggy outcrops, clean air and you'd be halfway there. It made you feel about an inch tall, surrounded by the massive majesty of nature. And in the middle of that— in the middle of a herd of goats," he added with a shadowy smile, "I finally had my answer."

"Give up Saint Catherine's."

He nodded. "I was working myself to death in a career I was beginning to hate." He gave a self-deprecating snort. "Hell, to be honest I'd never really enjoyed it, not the way I should've."

She nodded. Everything was beginning to make more sense. She'd thought he'd had the perfect family, the perfect career, but beneath that polish lurked so much more.

Just like her, really. AJ blinked and opened her mouth to say something, but he beat her to it.

"So, I'll pick you up tomorrow."

Tomorrow? What…? Oh. Her first appointment. "You're coming with me?"

A small frown creased his brow. "Why wouldn't I?"

"But I thought… What about..?" He confused her! He'd rearranged his schedule to be with her?

"This isn't something you should do alone." His gaze held hers. "I'll see you tomorrow," he said firmly, kissing her for one second, two, then getting out of the car and coming around to open the door for her and walk her inside.

From the foyer AJ watched him return to the car, then drive away, and the aching loss bit so deep her insides felt like they'd crumpled in on themselves. Which meant…

It meant she cared. Otherwise why had she gotten so riled about Katrina's attitude? Why had she been so affected by Matt's retelling of his past?

She cared what other people thought about her, about her relationship with Matt. She cared how other people saw him.

Her heart raced, breath catching painfully in her throat. She was falling for Matthew Cooper all over again.

Unbelievable. Absolutely unbelievable. What the hell was she supposed to do now?

With a sigh she tipped her gaze to the foyer ceiling and closed her eyes.

You'll do what you always do—suck it up and get through it. Because confessing her feelings? Making herself that open, that vulnerable again only to have Matt reject her?

That would kill her.

Fifteen

AJ had no idea how on earth women went through IVF over and over again. Every hope, every emotion was right there on the surface, raw and vulnerable. Handling all of that, plus the actual physical intrusion of the procedure, was way more than she'd bargained for. Thank God Matt had insisted on coming. His presence soothed her, his touch and low murmur of encouragement calmed her as the doctors efficiently went through the motions. His thumb gently stroked her knuckles, a rhythmic reassurance that gave her enough strength to suck everything up and ignore the pain, the uncertainty, the growing wave of doubt that battered her heart.

Hours later, aching and emotionally spent, she let him take her back to his apartment, remove her shoes and settle her on the sofa with a blanket and a cup of tea.

And when he made a move to leave, she grabbed his hand. "Stay with me."

They sat in silence on the sofa, his arms wrapped around her, her head on his chest as the familiar heat seeped into her very bones. Beneath her cheek his heart beat out a comforting rhythm, lulling her into a dangerous sense of contentment.

When the tears came, she didn't bother to wipe them away. He said nothing, but as his shirt slowly dampened his arms tightened around her, which only made the tears flow faster.

She had no idea why she was crying, but she did it silently, without movement, pretending he didn't know and couldn't feel the spreading wetness beneath her cheek. And he didn't let on, just held her, his hand gently stroking her arm over and over until, finally, she fell into an exhausted sleep.

AJ woke the next morning with gritty eyes and a dull ache in her gut.

She blinked, shifted and suddenly realized she was in a strange bed with a warm body pressed up against her back. A cozy lean body, his arm wrapped around her waist, his chin resting at the back of her neck.

Matt.

She vaguely remembered him guiding her into his bedroom, taking off her jacket and then her jeans, before putting her to bed dressed in just her knickers, bra and a blue tank top. A top that had shifted during the night and was now riding high on her rib cage.

A soft breath feathered across her shoulder and everything tightened, a crazy burst of desire and joy welling up in her throat. The reaction was so sudden, so shocking, that it floored her.

You want this. You want him.

Not just for now, not just for a limited time. Despite knowing who he was, how he lived his life and their checkered past, she wanted Matthew Cooper forever.

Her eyes squeezed shut as she tried to block out the tidal wave of emotion flooding in, tossing her high into the air only to leave her floundering as the waters receded.

You can't do this. You approached him. You started it. And now you have to deal with it.

He shifted suddenly, his thigh brushing against her bottom, and she felt another pang of yearning.

How desperately did she want this child? And was that desire enough to give her the strength to keep doing this for as long as it took, knowing that once she was pregnant, she and Matt would cease to be?

She had absolutely no clue.

He stirred again and this time his groin settled in the small of her back.

Oh, no. He was aroused, pressing firmly into her, and she was liking it too much.

His arm tightened around her waist, one hand splaying across her belly, and the intimate gesture short-circuited her brain. She couldn't move, couldn't think, just lay there stunned, her heart going crazy. Then she heard him suck in a deep breath, blowing it out slowly across the back of her neck.

"Angel."

That one sleepy, sexy word did her in.

She couldn't resist. She squeezed her eyes shut, then gently pushed her bottom back into his hardness and was rewarded with a soft groan. Slowly, she moved again but this time, his hand went to her hip, stilling her.

"Angel…" She loved the sound of his rough voice, the remnants of sleep still clinging to it.

"Matt."

"Could you not…?"

"Not what?" She shifted again but he had a firm grip. She couldn't move.

"Not do that."

"Why not?"

"Because you're killing me."

"You don't like it?"

"It's not that."

"Then what?"

She felt him sigh against her nape, the warmth stirring her hair and giving her goose bumps. She waited but he remained silent, and after a few agonizing seconds, she gently removed his hand from her hip and rolled over to face him.

He propped his hand under his cheek, studying her, and the pure vulnerability of the picture he presented had her entire body aching with longing. She leaned in and kissed his cheek, welcoming the roughness, the delicious, just-woken smell of his skin. He remained still, giving no indication of encouragement. But no rejection, either. That emboldened her to keep going, to trail soft kisses down his jaw then back up the other side, until she got to the corner of his mouth and she couldn't resist any longer.

AJ kissed him. Their lips were the only place their bodies touched and she called on every strand of patience not to jump on him. Instead, she seduced him using only her mouth: skimming his bottom lip, stopping briefly to nibble, before heading over to the other corner of his mouth. She traced the gentle curves with the tip of her tongue, a feathery lick that explored the erotic swell of his bottom lip until his warm breath began to pick up.

Oh, she still had it. With a triumphant grin she gently drew his bottom lip between her teeth and sucked. She was rewarded by a strangled moan. Her pulse kicked up and she kept going, languidly giving his mouth all the attention it deserved when what she really wanted to do was strip him naked and lick him all over.

Yet he remained still, letting her command the moment. Lips slid across lips, tongues mingled, at first gently, then with much more insistence. Finally, she eased back, belly pooling with heat as his languid eyes sought hers.

His dark, expressive eyes thrilled and aroused her every time he looked at her that way. Her breath raced and suddenly everything inside melted into a mess of tangled emotion.

"Angel…" His voice was thick and low. "I don't think we should—"

"Let me do this. Please."

She shifted, placing a hand on his shoulder and nudging him back. He went and she followed, bringing them together in a melding of skin and pounding blood. He was naked except for a pair of boxers, and she took untold satisfaction in having his hot flesh against hers. Firm chest, taut belly, lean waist. And his groin, now hard with arousal, pressing into hers.

She brought herself up so she was sitting on his thighs, leaning in.

Such a lean, compact body, without an inch of fat to mar the perfection. She swept her hand across his smooth chest, her palms brushing over first one dark nipple, then the other.

There it was, his swift intake of breath, dragging first in through his nose, then slowly exiting his parted mouth. She loved the way she, AJ Reynolds, had so much influence, knowing if she moved a certain way, kissed him in a particular spot, she could send his pulse racing or have him groan in pleasure.

He had the same effect on her.

Trailing her fingers over the smooth ridges of his abdomen, she went farther down, ringing his belly button then taking the path of the thin hairline that disappeared into his boxers.

He was aroused all right. She cupped him through the cotton, welcoming the thick, throbbing heat beneath her palm. When she glanced up to meet his gaze, those dark eyes were half-mast with passion, a muscle in his jaw working.

"You okay?"

"Yeah." It sounded like he'd been gargling sand and with a slow smile, she looped her thumbs into his waistband and slowly dragged his boxers down.

He sprang free, every hard, beautiful inch of him, and she was suddenly so overwhelmed with emotion that she had to bite her lip to gain control. She wrapped her hand around his thick length and was rewarded by Matt's sharp gasp.

He was hot and hard and she reveled in his velvety length, running her hand along it, pausing at the base, her fingers brushing the springy curls, before continuing back up.

"Angel…" Matt muttered, clenching a fist in the bedsheets. She stroked him again, her hands working magic on his aching manhood.

"Look at me."

At her soft command his eyes sprang open, focusing unsteadily on the ceiling, then slowly, down to where AJ was sprawled across his body.

He took in her disheveled red hair, pale skin, wide blue

eyes, the sensual curve of lips as she firmly and rhythmically kept him at full arousal with her hand.

Then her smile spread and slowly, deliberately she slid him into her hot, wet mouth and he nearly lost it right there.

His eyes rolled back in his head as the excruciating sensations flooded in, removing all thought, all feeling except her mouth, her tongue, her hand. His hips bucked involuntarily, pushing himself deeper, and she obliged, taking all of him, increasing her pace slowly, then with more authority, until he was on the edge in record time.

Finally, he tensed, tightening in one final thrust, and for one drawn-out second he couldn't breathe, couldn't think. Then with a deep guttural groan, he let himself go.

"Angel." She was on his lips, in his breath, under his skin. Everywhere.

It was as it should be.

He'd gone again. That much was obvious. AJ had woken to find a letter, then proceeded to torture herself with the many different ways she could say "I told you so."

He'd be gone at least ten days. Three days in Norway, followed by a side trip to Indonesia and China.

Ten long days.

So for her it was back to business as usual—walking, sketching, living a seemingly idyllic existence. The days dragged, agonizing days of worry and anticipation as she studiously followed Dr. Adams's advice and waited for a sign that the first procedure had taken. Thanks to a combination of hormones and her now-undeniable feelings, her head was a mess, always thinking, always worrying. Desperate to focus on something else, she sketched a bunch of pictures, managed to secure a stall at the Rocks Markets and then threw herself into organizing it. On the upside, it gave her a legitimate reason to distance herself from Matt when he finally returned, ensuring that her crazy, impossible thoughts were kept to a minimum.

He came back on a Saturday, and they spent a perfectly decent time having dinner at a small Italian restaurant in Concord. And as if their last night together had never been, he dropped her off without even once trying to make a move.

It was…a relief. And also frustrating.

And then he was gone again and she kept right on obsessing.

The day soon arrived when Zac's apartment was to be sold and Matt insisted she move back into his place. With no other choice available, she reluctantly agreed.

Just as she was about to walk out the door, Emily called to remind her the time for the open house tomorrow night had changed. AJ's hand was tight on the phone as she sat on a lounge chair arm and listened to her sister's usual enthusiasm with ever increasing gloom.

"So," Emily finally said. "What have you been up to? How's it going with that guy you mentioned?"

To AJ's horror she burst into tears. Then, when she stopped blubbering and attempted to gather at least some dignity, she ended up blurting everything out, from the surgery, to her fertility clinic issues, to Matt's involvement, to the wait for the results that were due later that day.

They both cried. After Emily alternately apologized for not knowing and scolded her for keeping secrets, she finally said, "Well, of course, you'll have to bring Matt to the showing."

AJ stared out the window at the bright afternoon sun piercing the white clouds, then at the Sydney skyline. "There's no 'of course' about it."

"Oh, my God, AJ, you have *got* to be kidding! The man is going to be the father of your child and we haven't even met him. He is a part of your life, regardless of this whole deal thing…which I think is ridiculous, by the way. You will damn well bring him, okay?"

AJ sighed. "He's in Tasmania right now, Em. But fine, I'll ask." She glanced at the clock. "I have to be downstairs. Talk later?"

"Sure. You call him now, okay?"

"Em…"

"Call him. I'm going to hang up then call you back. If your phone is not engaged, I'm going to be so pissed off."

AJ sighed. "Fine."

She clicked off, then dialed Matt's number.

The ease with which he said yes stunned her. "Shouldn't you check your schedule and get back to me?" she said, jamming the phone under her ear as she stared out onto the street, watching the slow-moving midafternoon traffic.

"I'm back tomorrow, AJ. What time?"

"Seven."

"Good. I can come straight from the airport."

So it was done. She placed the phone into her back pocket as a thousand different emotions rushed in to swamp her. Thanks to his work and her avoidance techniques, she hadn't seen him in… She calculated. A week. A whole entire week of not seeing those dark eyes, the softly curling hair she always itched to touch. His lean, capable body perfectly clad in a sharp suit. His smile and the way his eyes creased and that dimple emerged.

She swallowed and collapsed into the foyer sofa. God, her body ached.

It wasn't fair. None of it. She'd gotten over Matthew Cooper once before, but it seemed her luck had run out. No way would she escape the second time.

With a sigh she focused on getting her things back to Matt's apartment, determinedly shoving the inevitable clinic phone call to the bottom of her mental to do list. Matt had wanted to be there when she called but work had dictated otherwise. Instead, she'd promised to wait until he returned that night.

She couldn't wait that long.

Half an hour later, she stood in Matt's apartment, on the phone with Dr. Adams.

When she finally hung up, she collapsed into the sofa,

overwhelming loss choking off her breath, crushing her tiny sliver of hope.

She wasn't pregnant.

Dr. Adams had assured her they would try again and had made an appointment for next week.

She cast her eyes over her meager belongings in the middle of the room. A case, a shoulder bag, a folder full of sketches and a box of perishables—an echo of her former life, aeons ago, when she'd picked up and moved on a whim. A life wandering, searching. She'd done so much yet so little, avoiding commitment, connection, heartache. Yet she'd come full circle and returned to the one man who'd managed to make her feel, make her care. The only man who'd gotten under her skin.

She tipped her head down, tears prickling behind her eyes as her heart swelled with a deep, aching hunger.

Oh, God. I don't want to do this anymore. I can't.

She wasn't that strong, no matter how much Emily said she was. She desperately wanted a baby, more than anything she'd ever wanted before, but she couldn't break her own heart to get it. And if it was Matt's baby, she'd always be wanting something more, something she could never have.

Making a baby was all they'd agreed to and he'd never indicated it could be anything more. He wasn't hers, however much she wanted him.

She just couldn't do it anymore.

Matt arrived at Zac's apartment at six-thirty with a giddy sense of anticipation.

A week. Seven whole days. Sure, he'd been occupied with his crazy schedule, new clients and staff drama, but AJ was always in the back of his mind and surged to the front whenever there was downtime. Like on a long flight with only his thoughts for company. Or alone at night, when sleep refused to come.

In all the time he'd been away, she'd only called once. It

was obvious she was avoiding him and he knew exactly why. For all her bravado, all her tough outer shell, she was scared.

Yeah, he was, too. After his divorce, work was what he knew how to do and do well. Okay, so more than well. He knew how to give life back to those on death's door. Better, he gave hope, faith. Belief.

Yet he still didn't know how to break down the last of AJ's walls.

When he walked into the apartment and spotted her standing alone and to one side in the living room, Matt drank her in—heels, short black shirt, sheer bright blue top that draped off one shoulder—and fleetingly wondered what she'd do if he tossed her over his shoulder and just left.

Then she glanced up and a brief flash of something passed over her features before her mouth stretched into a smile. "Hi," she mouthed.

When she smiled like that…

He demolished the distance in seconds. "Hi yourself." Even though he'd decided not to push, he couldn't help leaning in to place a kiss on her mouth. He'd missed her too much.

Her surprised gasp warmed his lips. He smiled and pulled back. "Miss me?"

She blinked. "No."

He grinned. "Sure."

And suddenly, he was very much looking forward to tonight.

He looked good. Way too good. AJ didn't want to stare but she couldn't help herself, cataloging each feature: rough stubble dusting his chin, lean body in an impeccable black suit, skinny black tie and a sky-blue shirt.

Her heart began to beat a little faster when he smiled, hands jammed in his trouser pockets. He was…a rogue. That was it, a rogue with his rumpled sexy charm. He undid her a thousand different ways and she'd fallen all over again.

The conflict she'd been steadily building up all afternoon

suddenly became unbearable. Why hadn't she waited to call the clinic like she'd promised? She hated this, hated being the sole bearer of important news. It was exhausting. And because it was Matt, it made it a thousand times worse. Now she had to work out what she was going to say, pick the right time, then deal with his disappointment.

God, could this day get any worse?

He must have sensed something from her expression because his brows suddenly took a dive.

"AJ?"

The sound of someone clearing her throat had them both turning. Emily stood behind AJ, looking awkward. "Sorry, AJ, can I have a word?"

She opened her mouth to refuse, but something made her pause. Emily looked…weird. That was the only word for it. With a small frown, AJ nodded. "Sure."

Emily gave Matt a smile and said, "Hi, you must be Matt. Drinks are in the kitchen. We won't be long." Then she motioned for AJ to follow.

"What's up?" AJ asked when Emily led her into the bedroom and gently closed the door.

Emily took a breath, shoved a lock of curly brown hair behind her ear and threaded her fingers. "This is going to shock you.…"

"What?" AJ wasn't sure she could take any more bad news today.

"I got a call from our parents today."

"What?"

Emily winced. "They want to meet us."

"Like hell!" AJ yelled. "After all these bloody years—"

"Shh," Emily hissed, her gaze darting to the door.

"After all these years," AJ continued in a furious whisper. "After *nothing*. Not a single call, email, letter, whatever, and they make contact now? What, did they see your photo in the paper and think you're a convenient ATM now that you're married to a billionaire?"

At Emily's twisted expression, AJ knew the thought had occurred to her, too. She shook her head as fury bubbled its way to the surface. "Tell them they can go take a running jump. No—" she swallowed a thick breath "—I'll tell them myself."

"AJ," Emily said softly, grasping her hand. "I told them the decision was up to you. And if you want to do it, then I'll go with you."

A wave of fierce protectiveness swept over her. She'd rather walk on hot coals than see those two people again, but damned if she'd let them invade Emily's life. "Fine," she choked out and grabbed the door. "I need a drink. You call them, then let me know when and where."

With that, she swung the door wide and blindly stalked down the hall. This could not be happening! Just like that, the tainted memories surged, ripping into those solid walls she'd built around her past.

She stormed into the kitchen, startling Matt.

He turned, glass of wine in his hand, but with one look at her expression his smile disappeared. "What's wrong?"

Oh, God, where to start? Her eyes went to the ceiling. "Nothing."

"AJ, look at me." She reluctantly met his eyes, then just as quickly looked away. "Tell me what the problem is."

She couldn't. She just…couldn't. She could share her body with him, maybe even admit her feelings, but her past? Those awful, shameful years she'd tried her best to forget, burying them under a lifetime of parties, partners and spur-of-the-moment decisions?

No.

Instead, she fell back on the one thing that had been front and center up until ten minutes ago.

"I called the clinic today. The pregnancy didn't take."

A mixture of emotions passed over his face—shock, disappointment, sadness. Everything she'd experienced and more. It didn't make it any easier knowing he was affected by this, too.

"You didn't have to be alone for that."

Nausea welled in the face of his concern, the deep thread of guilt overshadowing everything.

She glanced over his shoulder, at the slowly growing gathering, and felt claustrophobia claw at her chest. "I need some air. I should—"

"AJ." She gasped when he grabbed her arms. "That's not all, is it?" His gentle tone, instead of soothing, only served to restoke her anger.

She twisted out of his grip. "It's nothing."

"Then why are you so angry?"

She glared. "That is none of your business, all right?"

He pulled back as if she'd slapped him, his eyes going wide before they suddenly narrowed. "Right. Because I'm only good for one thing."

"I didn't... You're—"

"Oh, no, I get it. Everything's off-limits except what you want and the occasional times we end up in bed," he ground out, his hands going into his pockets with a disgusted snort. "Frankly, I'm getting a little sick of it, AJ."

She stilled. "What are you saying?"

"I'm saying I'm sick of the restrictions. That I'm only allowed to have a part of you. That I'm not supposed to ask questions or bring up the past or even bloody well care about you! *That's* what I'm saying."

She blinked. "You care about me?"

"And that comes as a surprise? AJ, you have no clue, do you?"

"Why? Why would you care, Matt? You don't know me—"

"I know you better than you think."

"Oh, you do? You know nothing." She choked down a sob. "You don't know about my life, about my crappy parents, their drunken binges, their—"

"Can you stop that? You're *not* a sum of your childhood." He sighed. "AJ. Look, I know the news about the pregnancy is disappointing. But we can try again."

Her heart broke, and she felt the force of it reverberate

through every bone. She couldn't do this, not on top of everything else. "I need you to go."

"Why?"

Because I am totally in love with you and you're killing me. "Just go. Please."

His eyes held hers, furious and confused, until she was sure she'd burst into tears any second.

"Fine," He finally sighed. "I'll talk to you at home."

She shook her head. "No, I'm going to get a hotel room."

She'd stunned him and for a second he absorbed the blow, his eyes creasing in confusion. He looked as if he was about to say something but broke off with a disgusted snort.

Then he spun on his heel and stalked out the front door.

Sixteen

It was three on Sunday afternoon and AJ sat with Emily at City Extra in the Quay, both silently watching the bustle of Sydneysiders and tourists passing by on their way to ferries or the Museum of Contemporary Art or simply strolling around and enjoying the sun.

AJ's gut pitched, matching the churning waves in the pier opposite the restaurant. Apprehension, fear and anger all played a part in her emotional turmoil, yet her focus was on her argument with Matt, not on the impending family reunion.

Damn, it was just like before. No—way, way worse. Because now she knew him better and despite every wall she'd built, every warning, she'd gone and fallen in love and now her heart was breaking.

No, that wasn't right. How could her heart break when it was never whole to start with? She was damaged, scarred. She'd done far too much and seen far too many things to be anything other than a product of her broken childhood.

"AJ?"

She turned her attention from her untouched coffee to look up into Emily's concerned blue eyes.

"Are you sure about this?" Her sister reached for her hand. "After everything that's happened, you don't have to do this now. I can just—"

"Oh no." Her fingers wound around Emily's and she winced. "Sorry. But there's no way I'd leave you to do this on your own."

"You had a negative result," Emily pointedly reminded her. "Your body needs to rest."

AJ lifted one eyebrow. "Do you honestly think lying in bed is going to work for me?"

Emily was silent for a second before she shook her head. "We need to do this, don't we?"

"Yeah. But I wish—"

Emily's gaze slid past her shoulder. Her eyes widened, and her face went pale. A sudden roar of blood pounded in AJ's ears as a female voice cut through the chatter of the Sunday crowds.

"Emily! Baby! It's you!"

AJ jumped to her feet and whirled around so fast her chair flew back.

It was their mother, no doubt about it. She was painfully skinny, poured into a pair of white jeans and a leopard-print tank top. Her outfit only emphasized her thin arms and nonexistent waist. But what was more noticeable, past the frizzy red hair, huge gaudy diamante sunglasses and a dozen gold rings and bangles that jangled alarmingly, were the deep grooves bracketing her thin, pink-painted mouth.

"And Angelina Jayne!" Charlene Reynolds declared loudly, raising her sunglasses to her hair and placing her hands on those bony hips. "Girls, you both look absolutely gorgeous!" Her eyes briefly skimmed over AJ before snapping back to Emily, and when that sharp, assessing gaze lingered a little too long on Emily's curvy hips with a brief frown, AJ felt the anger simmer in earnest.

Then she glanced past their gaudily clad birth mother and her gut pitched alarmingly. "Keith?"

"Hi there, Red."

AJ's eyes met Emily's, reflecting her surprise. "You two are still together?"

"Amazing, right?" Her stepfather looked downright respectable in his chinos, checkered shirt and loafers but she knew he was anything but. He'd always reminded AJ of a stereotypical car salesman, a guy whose eyes never met yours, whose oily grin grated on people's nerves, whose fast talk and cheap ways made him more enemies than friends. No wonder they'd had to move so often.

When his arm snaked around Charlene's waist and he planted a kiss smack bang on her mouth, AJ wanted to gag. "Me and Charl, we're just meant to be."

AJ looked back at Emily, who'd been silent and pale for too long. Now she coughed and indicated the table. "Will you sit?"

Charlene nodded her approval and took the seat on AJ's left—which left Keith directly to her right.

"So, girls," she began with a wide smile, arms crossed on the table. "It's wonderful to see you two again after all these years."

"How…?" AJ cleared her throat, then started again. "How did you find us?"

She ignored Emily's frown and instead focused on the woman who had made her life hell for the first twelve years of her life.

The years had not been kind to her mother, with the creases continuing around the older woman's eyes and forehead—not lines born from laughter, sun and joy, but ones AJ knew were the product of drugs, alcohol and awful life choices. Her blue eyes looked tired, yet her assessment of AJ was shrewd and she knew Charlene was forming an unflattering opinion behind that silent scrutiny.

"Well, sweetheart, we saw Emily's wedding photo in the paper, didn't we?" She barely glanced at Keith for confirmation. "What a beautiful dress! And that new husband of yours…" She paused theatrically. "Well, if I were ten years younger—"

"Look, what do you want, Charlene?"

Charlene blinked and focused on AJ, her mouth pursing. "That's not very polite, Angelina."

"My name is AJ."

"Your birth certificate says Angelina, sweetheart." She

blew out a scoffing chuckle, glancing at Emily, then Keith. "What kind of a name is AJ?"

"One I *like*."

Charlene's eyes narrowed. "Well, I *don't*."

"Well, I *don't care*."

Charlene's hand suddenly twitched and even though it had been more than fifteen years, AJ felt the familiar burn of fear and defiance in her stomach. She braced herself, back straightening even though her head screamed *Move!*

Her vision narrowed, focusing on that one small movement, ready for the blow that would come, would always come.

"Charlene," Keith said hastily, putting a hand on the older woman's clenched fists. "This isn't the best way to start our reunion, not after all these years."

Charlene's eyes sparked, throat working as the anger lines thinned her mouth. AJ glared her down, furious flames banking in her belly. *I'm not ten anymore. She can't hurt me now. I'm not about to back down.*

"You're right, Keith," Charlene finally said, dripping saccharine. She gave AJ a death glare before turning her overly bright smile on Emily. "Sweetheart, I can't tell you how proud I am—how we both are—that you've done so well for yourself. Who would've thought my little Emily would end up marrying a *Preston?*" She reverently breathed out the last word, her hand to her throat.

"You want money," AJ blurted out.

Charlene's eyes snapped back to AJ. "What?"

"I said, you want money." AJ leaned back in her chair and crossed her arms. "This isn't some impromptu reunion. You saw Emily's photo, saw who she'd married and thought you could score a freebie."

Charlene's mouth opened, then quickly slammed shut. "That's not a very nice thing to say."

"True, though."

AJ eyed Charlene's hands as they slowly curled into fists, then just as slowly flattened on the table.

"No, Angelina, it's not. Look, you want the truth?" She leaned in, her expression earnest. "I've been looking for both of you for years. I even have my name on a bunch of registers to find you. You can check if you like."

AJ saw a mix of confusion and disbelief in Emily's wide blue eyes and felt protective anger burn the back of her throat. Emily never could hide her feelings. And they'd see that confusion and play on it. Even now, Keith was studying her with a cool calculation that made AJ furious.

"What. A load. Of crap," AJ said succinctly, taking no small satisfaction as everyone's eyes darted back to her.

Charlene took a deep, aggrieved breath. "Listen, Angelina—"

"No, *you* listen." AJ leaned in, fury making her entire body shake. "You abandoned us. I was in the hospital, recovering from surgery, and you *left me there.* Emily was ten years old and had to catch public transport on a Saturday night to find me."

"Angelina, if you'd just—"

"Oh, are you going to tell me it wasn't your fault? That you can't help yourself, that it's the booze, the drugs or whatever loser friends you had at the time?" She raked her gaze over Charlene. "Why don't you just admit you're a pathetic woman and an awful mother and save us both the effort?"

"I never said I was perfect!"

AJ snorted. "I would've settled for decent."

Charlene's expression twisted, her gaze contemptuous. "Yeah, well, I never did want either of you in the first place," she spat. "And you—you're just as bad as your father. That selfish bastard had a mouth on him, too."

AJ glared at the woman who'd given birth to her, the same woman who should have loved and protected her but instead had used and abused her power. She'd conditioned AJ to lie and steal to support Charlene's drug habit. She'd abandoned them both in a public hospital with no clothes, no home and no money.

Finally, after all these years drifting, searching, secretly wishing for something, someone who could make her believe she deserved much more than she'd been born into, she had her answer.

I'm free.

AJ stood, suddenly desperate to leave. "You don't know me, Charlene. You never have." She shoved her chair under the table, noting with satisfaction that Emily was following suit. "Nothing you could say could hurt me because that'd mean I care what you think—and I don't." She dragged her gaze from Charlene's furious expression to her sister. "Em? Shall we go?"

"Sweetheart." Charlene placed a hand over Emily's and squeezed, making her wince. "If you would just hear me out—"

God bless her sister because she yanked her hand away and stood staring down at their mother with a look that could only be described as pity. AJ sent up a silent cheer when their eyes met over Charlene's teased hair and they both gave an imperceptible nod.

AJ grinned. *Love you, Em.*

Emily grinned back. *Love you more, AJ.*

"Wait!" Keith grabbed AJ's wrist. "You can't—ooooof!"

AJ's elbow connected with his chest and she couldn't deny the deep satisfaction his yelp gave her. "You, Keith, are a slimy douche bag who can't keep his hands to himself, either above or below the table."

And with that, she took Emily's hand and they walked out into the sun.

Someone was knocking.

AJ paused in her packing and glanced at her hotel door. It came again.

With a sigh she went over, placing her eye up to the peep-hole. Instantly, she pulled back with a soft murmur.

"AJ, open the door."

She shook her head silently.

"I know you're there."

Still she waited, her cheek on the cool door as she held her breath.

"Please, Angel."

Oh, God. She bit down on her lip, choking off a groan. She'd booked a late-afternoon flight, had rehearsed what she was going to say when she called him from the airport. Yet all that preparation felt somehow inadequate, like she wasn't giving him her full attention.

You can't leave it like this.

With a deep breath, she gathered her composure, pulled her shoulders back and slowly unlocked the door.

He stood there, gorgeous as always in his business suit, and for one second she wanted to launch herself at him, kiss him senseless and confess everything.

She couldn't.

"Paige called me," he said. "Your phone's been off and you missed your date."

Oh, damn. AJ rubbed the bridge of her nose. "I forgot."

"She's worried about you." He tipped his head, dark eyes searching her face. "So am I." He glanced past her. "Can I come in?"

She stepped back, allowing him entry. When he strode past she managed to suck his smell deep into her lungs before reluctantly breathing out again.

You can do this. You have to do this.

He turned in the middle of the room but not before he took in her open suitcase on the bed. Instead of grilling her about that, he said, simply, "Emily also called me."

"Oh?"

"She told me you met your parents yesterday."

What? She clenched her jaw. "Why would she do that?"

"Because she's worried about you, too."

AJ sighed. "I just... I think—" She broke off with a frown, stuck her hands in her back pockets and released a slow breath.

She didn't have to tell him, but she'd come too far now *not* to tell him. She was sick of keeping all this crap inside, sick of having it affect everything she did.

She sighed and slumped into the sofa. "My mother was awful. She partied, drank, took drugs. She and whatever guy she was with were neglectful and selfish, moving from one housing commission to another, trashing the places before skipping out on the rent. They also took great delight in training my sister and me to steal from a very early age. I was arrested a few times."

Shame ripped through her body, the very action of verbalizing it tearing her from the inside out. But something made her continue.

"I was sixteen when my appendix burst. I came out of surgery to find my sister clinging onto the bed rail with child services trying to drag her away.

"Thanks to the Young Offenders Act, it didn't go through the courts—there was mediation, liaison, all that stuff. My parents sat there like contrite model citizens, nodded sagely and expressing their desire to change and be better, while a DOCS worker outlined the issues. They had everyone fooled. Except…" She swallowed, the sting of embarrassment still familiar after all these years. Yet Matt's concerned expression forced her to go on, to finally air the dirty little secrets she'd kept so close to her heart. "One cop. He suspected something was wrong. And when they realized he was digging around, they did a runner."

"They left you?"

She nodded. "A warrant was issued, but because it wasn't considered a major crime, the police had to wait until they crossed back over to Western Australia. Which they never did."

"So what happened?"

AJ shrugged. "Emily went into foster care and I moved to Sydney. Did lots of jobs up and down the coast. Met you. Then I found Emily years later and we reconnected. I…" She scowled, recalling the stupid beliefs that had kept her from her sister for so long. "I thought she'd be better off without me. Plus I couldn't deal with the guilt of leaving her, the questions she'd ask. It was just too much and I didn't want to face it."

She fell silent, studying her nails with determined scrutiny as the memories washed over her. But when the silence stretched, she glanced up. Matt was staring at her, those dark eyes so direct, so firm that she felt the urge to just blurt everything out, put it all out there.

Then he glanced over at her suitcase and the moment was gone. "So you're leaving, then."

She nodded.

His face was expressionless. "I see."

"Don't you want to know why?"

He shoved his hands in his pockets. "Obviously, you've changed your mind about having a baby."

Oh, how easy if that was the true reason. She searched his face with a growing sense of desperation. *Get angry. Yell at me. Anything that would justify my decision.*

He just stared back, waiting.

Instead, he ran his hand through his hair, his eyes softening. "AJ, I'm sorry about yesterday's results. But we can try again—"

"No." She shook her head. "I'm done."

He looked confused. "But this was just the first time. Why—?"

"Because I can't do it anymore."

"Again, why?"

God, she wished he wouldn't look at her that way.

"AJ, just tell me."

Her eyes darted away. "Look, I just don't think it's fair on you to keep doing this. You have a career, a life. One day you'll want to get married again and I don't—"

"Don't you do that. Don't make me the reason, AJ. That's not fair. You tell me what you want without making me the excuse for walking out."

Matt's heart pounded as a terrible fear coursed through his blood. She stood there, still and small with the burden of truth he'd laid on her, and for one heart-stopping second everything teetered on the edge, threatening to crash and burn.

She took a deep breath. "Fine." She crossed her arms, the protective gesture revealing the depth of her doubt. "In a perfect world I want what anyone wants. A baby. A partner. A life full of laughter and love and joyous moments. But it's not a perfect world. I have to face the reality that I'll probably never have kids. I don't want to spend months—years—being poked and prodded only to have the results turn out negative every time. It…" She stared at the floor for the longest time. "It's breaking me and I can't do it."

"AJ…" His voice croaked and he coughed to clear it.

"What do you want, Matt?" She addressed the floor still, and the vulnerability of her stance, in her soft words, wounded him.

This was it. His moment of truth.

He'd rehearsed it over and over in his head. It all came down to this. A terrible fear froze his lungs. *Don't stuff it up.*

But when he opened his mouth, all that came out was, "I want you to stay."

She looked up cautiously.

"You had your clarity six months ago. I had mine when Jack died." He moved closer and she tipped her head up, her eyes wide and riddled with confusion as she met his gaze. "I spent years building a career. I married someone exactly like me and we were driven by success and the need to achieve. But after Jack died, I realized I couldn't do it any longer. I wanted more. I wanted a life. A family. When I asked Katrina, she refused point-blank to consider it." The memory made his jaw clench, but he quickly brushed it away. "I—"

"Are you saying you want a *baby?*"

When he nodded, she crossed her arms and leaned back, staring and openmouthed.

"You've known this all along," she said tightly.

He nodded again and this time she shook her head, one hand pushing away a stray curl. "And these past few weeks have been...what? A way to seduce me?"

"Not exactly..."

She blinked slowly, her eyes never leaving his. "Why, Matt? Why would you do that?"

"Because I was an idiot ten years ago and I let you go. I didn't want to make the same mistake again. AJ..." He took a step toward her. "I haven't stopped thinking about you. Even in the middle of a job, I've been thinking about you."

A soft sound gurgled in her throat as her eyes widened.

"I love you, AJ," he continued, then took her hands, holding them between his warm fingers. "I've always loved you. And I don't want to lose you again."

It felt like the world had stopped spinning in that moment, that everything depended on what she said next. He held his breath, waiting, until her eyes closed briefly, as if it pained her somehow. His heart raced, hanging on the edge, waiting for her response.

"But why...?" She cleared her throat. "Why didn't you just say something?"

He snorted. "Oh, yeah. Sure. You ask me to father a child without strings and I tell you I love you? You would've hit the door running."

AJ couldn't think. Couldn't breathe. Through her deafening heartbeat, through every muscle, every vein screaming in joy, she realized her fingers were trembling.

If she cried now, she wouldn't know how to stop.

Damn it. She was crying.

Matt's expression softened as he stood and she felt the tears flow even faster.

"Angel..." he choked out, stroking a tender thumb across her cheek. "Does this mean you're sad?"

She pressed her lips together, vehemently shaking her head. "I just...I just..."

"Shhh," he squeezed her hands. "Take a breath. Start again."

She did as he suggested, dragging air into her lungs once, then twice, as he brushed the tears from her other cheek.

Then he cupped her face and she became completely, totally undone.

"Do you know how long I've been waiting to say something?" she finally whispered. "All the times we were together, it killed me but I didn't want to stop because I needed to see you again."

He went still, his wide brown eyes searching hers.

"Matt, I didn't want to. I told myself not to. But I fell in love with you and I—"

His mouth cut off the rest of her words.

Yes. His lips slid across hers in a searing kiss. AJ met the full force of his passion and need and gave him back more, wrapping her arms around his neck, bringing him closer, as her heart swelled with total and complete joy. This was too much. She didn't deserve this.

And yet here it was. He wanted her. Matthew Cooper *loved* her.

When they finally broke apart, hot and breathless, AJ sighed. "Matt...are you sure? I mean, really, really sure?" She glanced away from his silent study. "Because you know my chances of having a baby aren't good."

"Angel, just because you might not be able to physically bear a child doesn't mean I don't love you any less. If you want to keep trying, I'll support you. If you want to adopt, I'll support you. Okay?"

Again with the tears. And when he leaned in and placed a tender kiss on her mouth, her heart collapsed.

God, she loved this man! Loved every frustrating, intense, wonderful inch of him. She covered his hands with her own and leaned into the kiss, wanting more, wanting everything.

"I love you, Matt."

She felt his mouth curve against hers. "And I love you, too,

Angel. You're more important to me than anything else. I'm going to delegate some of my work so I can spend time with you building our family. And if I have to travel anywhere to serve my clients, you'll be with me. As my wife."

Wife?

Her surprise must've shown because his soft laugh suddenly broke the silence.

"I want to marry you," he murmured. "Is that so surprising?"

Totally. But instead, she just shook her head. "Not at all."

"Liar. You are totally surprised."

She shook her head with a small smile. "A little."

"Well, believe it. Angelina Jane Reynolds..." He looped his arms around her waist, his expression deadly serious. "Will you marry me?"

For this decision, she didn't even need to think. "In a heartbeat."

Epilogue

Three months later, AJ stood at the entrance to the wedding marquee in the Palazzo Versace's private function area, silently panicking inside. A thousand different emotions competed for attention, yet it was overwhelming joy that gripped the most tightly.

Emily handed her the white rose bouquet as Paige busily adjusted her skirts. The cream wedding dress fit to perfection, with its sweetheart neckline, the tight beaded bodice that accented her waist and the skirts that swept down to the floor, parting in front to reveal rich sky-blue satin decorated with starbursts and sequined butterflies.

It was beautiful. She felt beautiful.

When she glanced up, she found herself the entire focus of the crowd and her heart suddenly started to beat double time.

"Don't worry," Emily whispered. "You look gorgeous. And your soon-to-be husband doesn't look too bad himself."

AJ's gaze automatically went down the aisle, where the celebrant and best man stood. But she had eyes only for Matt.

He was dressed in an old-style sandy-colored smoking suit, a pristine white shirt and a shiny blue cravat that matched the lining of her dress. His hair brushed his collar, and his chin was dusted with thin stubble. When those dark eyes fixed on her, then creased in appreciation, everything disappeared.

God, she loved him.

She wanted to sprint down that aisle, grab his hand and run away with him. Instead, she focused on his face, the breathless emotion in his eyes, the grin that spread as she put one foot in front of the other, surely and steadily, until they were finally side by side.

It felt like hours, but in reality, it only took a few seconds to reach him.

He leaned down, lips close to her ear. "You look amazing."

She smiled back, linking her fingers through his when he offered his hand. "So do you."

"Are you ready for this?"

"Yes." She glanced around at their small party, then back to him. "And I hope you're ready for next month, too."

He gave her a quizzical look. "What's next month?"

She bit her lip, unable to contain her cool composure any longer. "Elise from the adoption agency called. They've approved us. This time next week, we'll be parents."

His smile got even wider, to the point where it nearly blinded her. Ignoring all the guests, the celebrant, the hotel staff and a handful of onlookers, he swooped down for a kiss.

"Matt!" she laughingly protested against his mouth. "We haven't said our vows yet."

"I don't care. This is a kissing moment and I'm taking it."

And in that one moment, with the sound of the crowd's laughter ringing around them, AJ had everything she could possibly want.

* * * * *

Don't miss Emily and Zac's story,
PROMOTED TO WIFE?
by Paula Roe,
available as an ebook
from Harlequin Desire.

MILLS & BOON®

Why not subscribe?
Never miss a title and save money too!

Here's what's available to you if you join the
exclusive **Mills & Boon Book Club** today:

✦ *Titles up to a month ahead of the shops*
✦ *Amazing discounts*
✦ *Free P&P*
✦ *Earn Bonus Book points that can be redeemed
  against other titles and gifts*
✦ *Choose from monthly or pre-paid plans*

Still want more?
Well, if you join today we'll even give you
50% OFF your first parcel!

So visit **www.millsandboon.co.uk/subs**
or call Customer Relations on 020 8288 2888
to be a part of this exclusive Book Club!